DEAD SHIP DOWN

Robert W. Walker

DEAD SHIP DOWN

DOUBLE DRAGON

From the author of Titanic 2012, Bismarck 2013
& The Chicaghosts Series

CHAPTER ONE

"Something's alive on the Andrea Doria!" -- Dr.
Jenna Corey

"Death is nothing at all...I have only
slipped away into the next room...I am I,
and you are you...whatever we were to
each other that we are still."
— Henry Scott Holland 1847-1918

The Andrea Doria had slipped under the waves
after listing to starboard, lying like an enormous
skyscraper on its side, and now at the bottom of the
North Atlantic, she likewise was intact and lying on
her side. She did not look like the caved-in, ripped
apart, pancaked inward shipwrecked Titanic but
more like the intact Bismarck. But the Andrea Doria
was a shipwreck that could be gotten to by divers
trained in deep water dives, whereas Titanic and
Bismarck were not within diving distance by any
stretch of the imagination, despite films and books
to the contrary. They were thousands of feet out of
reach except by submarine. Even then a diver could
not truly inspect these ships, unable to 'dive' into
the Titanic.

But here, above the Italian cruise liner, Andrea
Doria, two more divers slowly descended, properly,
cautiously, as trained. Between them, they had
15,345 hours of dive experience but only 5000 of

7

that was in the kind of deep depths where they now headed. They'd come equipped with the best communications, lights, tanks, and confidence. They w

ere diving the Mt. Everest of shipwrecks, the Andrea Doria, some sixty miles off the coast of Nantucket and 200 feet below the surface.

"I know you're anxious to get to the ship and search the interior, Jake," Jenna Corey said into her com-link as she descended just ahead of Jake Stoughton, holding him up. "But I'm already feeling a bit queasy, so just cool your jets."

"Cool my jets. Haven't heard that expression since high school." Jake held onto the guideline, a strong hemp line that went from the dive boat, Explorer II to the wreck below. The line had been secured to a buoy that marked the dive location left by the last tour boat that had come and gone with anxious divers who wanted a look at the remains of the Andrea Doria. The Explorer II, however, was no excursion boat but a ship dedicated to ocean exploration and sometimes salvage operations, if a salvage operation appeared lucrative.

Still most who came out to dive the famous cruise liner came on tour boats. This usually meant ten or twelve divers of various ages and backgrounds from all over the states and the world who wanted to be able to say that they'd kneeled on the deck of this particular shipwreck. Due to Doria's reputation, the shipwreck drew divers like flies. A reputation as the most dangerous shipwreck dive of them all. It certainly had earned that reputation with seventeen divers who'd not returned alive from her deck.

Descending took time and aside from the Trimix of air they breathed, time was their most precious commodity down here. Still, if Jenna was feeling woozy or lightheaded, she might do well to slowly return to the dive boat now. The pressures at these depths played havoc on the human body.

Jake advised her to turn and start up, adding, "I can manage alone."

"I'm OK, Jake."

"If I locate Pritchards' body inside Doria, we still have two more days on site."

"No…no, I'm fine. Just needed a minute."

"You sure?"

"Yes, now quit harping, Jake."

"You know damn well down here we can't be too careful. Seventeen divers dead ahead of you, kiddo."

She said no more, moving down the guideline instead of up. Clenching onto the heavy rope with the idling boat and the powerful current tearing at it, made holding on difficult. If not careful, the rope could tear loose a glove and rip skin down to bone. No one wanted blood in the water, not out here in the North Atlantic.

They continued their descent to the shipwreck. Like any death investigation, the first step was to have a look at the body and its surroundings, to scope out the site where the victim was last seen alive. Just because Thom Pritchards' body remained unaccounted for, that was no reason to assume his body could not be found inside or near the wreck. Both Jenna and Jake had to assume that the unfortunate sixty-four-year old, veteran diver—or what was left of him—could be found. He has to be down here somewhere, Jake thought. Quite possibly inside the shipwreck.

Most of the now seventeen divers who'd perished in, around, and on the deck of the Andrea Doria had perished inside the wreck, lured in, no doubt by some shiny object, a peek through a portal, or some notion that one more minute inside the hulking wreck would net a quick fortune, a find like no other. Riches always presented a lure difficult to race away from even if a man had only a few minutes left of his oxygen mix. One of the dead, a fellow named Dennis Goreman of Pensacola, Florida was found clutching some cheap rosary beads he'd found somewhere in the wreck. Like many of the others, Goreman was a top-notch diver, a veteran who should not have died inside this wreck. But Goreman had no rich relatives putting up a small fortune for his recovery.

Not all but some of the bodies of those who'd died here had been recovered and autopsied. Cause of death ranged from heart attack to the bends—from ascending or descending too fast. Some who'd perished were thought to be suicidal as they had not been in good health or in any shape to make the dive in the first place. Others had gone down without sufficient training in deep water diving. After all, the ship was slightly over 250 feet below the surface at its stern. Most recreational divers seldom went beyond sixty feet, and to go even to 150 required special equipment and special mix of three gases in one's tanks called a Trimix.

Jake and Jenna had been hired by the Richards children and estate to recover Thom Richards' remains, and they'd been paid a wonderful advance, plus a sizable donation to the cause of dive safety for which Jake tirelessly worked.

The 'recovery' dive had been meticulously planned. Jenna had interviewed one of the divers who'd gone down with Richards, and Jake had interviewed the other man. They'd also interviewed a couple, man and wife, who'd come up after Richards' dive buddies who might have seen something. The couple recalled having seen a strobe light like their own attached to the guideline, and the initials on the strobe light, a beacon to guide a diver back to the rope and the surface, read: TR—Thom Richards. Presumably, Richards had not gotten back to the guideline, despite the fact, his two dive partners had believed him right behind them on their ascent to the dive boat that day, the Whahoo.

"Another reason to believe the man had turned back, curious about something, despite his running low on his Trimix. By the time a diver got to this depth, he only had a mere fifteen minutes at the wreck site before he must ascend and switch over to normal oxygen as he did so.

For some reason, Richards failed to do anything approximating protocol down here. Aside from the monetary motive, Jenna and Jake wanted to know

11

why, and how could it happen to so many veteran divers? There were diving deaths all across the globe, and most were associated with shipwreck dives. But no shipwreck had claimed a fraction of the lives that Andrea Doria had taken.

Was there an explanation? Or would the mystery remain forever a mystery?

"The depth has all to do with it," Jake insisted during their planning stage.

"I know but that's just one factor, Jake. I have a sixth sense that there's more to it. Something simply not right."

"Don't tell me you think the ship's haunted." He'd laughed after the scoff.

"Haunted, perhaps not, but Jake haunting, now that's another story."

"How do you mean?"

"You know how people go to the Grand Canyon of the Yellowstone and throw themselves to their deaths there?"

"I've read about that. Yeah, a lot of people choose it to end it all."

"Like the Golden Gate Bridge. Some places just somehow lure people to their deaths. The haunting is inside them, not outside…or you might see it as a combination of the two."

"A shipwreck like a bridge entices people to suicide, sure. I get that. The beauty of the canyon, I get it. But this is an ugly heap of metal on the ocean floor."

"But from everything his friends, dive buddies, children, wife said about him, Richards loved life

12

and had never suffered from depression," she had argued. "Then he sees Doria for the first time and he's mesmerized."

"You may have something there, but it's kinda far-fetched."

"Not really. What if he got a diagnosis—say cancer or Alzheimer's onset—everyone's worst nightmare? And he told no one?"

Jake had scratched his head. "I suppose anything's possible, but suicide by shipwreck is a new one on me."

"Just sayin' it's a possibility."

"You know people better'n I ever will. I bow to your thinking, Dr. Corey."

They now arrived at the shipwreck and snapped on their strobe lights to the guide rope. The strobe lights sent out a signal of light that could be seen for some fifty yards. Their much stronger lights attached to their shoulders penetrated the length of a football field topside in the dark, but in the murky waters here, they were lucky to get half that. In the distance, as they continued to follow the guideline attached to the hull of the ship, they first saw the reflection of coral reef growing on the wreck. Curious fish, some that'd made a home of the wreck came into view along with a scuttling crab here and there.

Suddenly, the outline of the ghostly ship itself came into focus. It was, as shipwrecks go, both huge and elegant in its demise. Many a shipwreck dive was over a structure one quarter the size of the famous Italian cruise liner Andrea Doria. This was far closer to diving the Titanic—a ship thousands of feet below the surface, miles below, and out of the reach of shipwreck divers. This was the closest thing to accomplishing that miracle. Every time Jake saw it, the Andrea Doria struck a place in his heart. "She's as beautiful as ever," he muttered into his com-link.

Above on Explorer II, Sam 'Sharky' Kent replied, "I hear that. Tomorrow, I'm coming with you guys for a look."

"You're welcome, Sam," said Jake. "Once you're feeling better."

Sam had picked up a bug that had him barfing half way out from Woods Hole.

"She is such a sad beauty," Jenna then said, staring at the lines of the huge ship that had lain here since her sinking in 1956. The entire hull and deck was covered with sea life and ruinous rusticles—a term for the oxidation of metal coined by Bob Ballard, the Woods Hole scientist who had discovered the whereabouts of both the Titanic and the Bismarck on the floor of the North Atlantic.

Since the Andrea Doria was at a depth of hundreds of feet rather than thousands, and since it was on the continental shelf, more sea life existed in and around her. She had become a huge reef for the sea creatures.

"When you guys tire of admiring the shipwreck," began Sam, "you can get busy searching for Richards…or what's left of him. He's been under water somewhere now for six months."

14

"Do you have us on camera, Sam?" asked Jenna, who had talked of creating a documentary about this 'expedition', even kicking over a title: Dive Into Death. That was a long way off, but footage of each day's search for Richards, with the possibility of finding others who'd disappeared here over the years, made the idea titillating. She'd hoped to get the backing of Woods Hole and Jake's bosses at the University of Rhode Island, URI. All of it was in the talk stages for now.

Sam assured Jenna that all cameras were operating just fine.

"Shall we split up. We only have fourteen minutes left," Jenna said to Jake.

"Now we talked about this. We should stay close."

"Close then, but you take the left stairwell down, and I'll take the right."

"Jenna…"

"Time is of the essence, Jake. We need to be successful here."

"Alright but stay in contact."

Jake made his way into the bowels of the ship to the left, descending a stairwell at his right. The stairs went from the top deck to a corridor below. Jenna did the same, going down the left stairwell and into the corridor there. They had studied the schematics of the ship until they knew every nook and cranny, but the reality was that once inside, nothing looked as it did on blueprints and drawings.

"I'm going to find the gymnasium, check it out," Jake said just to keep in touch with her.

Jenna laughed lightly and replied, "You think Richards stayed for a workout?"

"Men are drawn to the smell of sweat. What can I tell ya?"

"Try out the rings maybe, the horse while you're in there. Might do you some good."

They were silent for some time, in search and rescue mode when Jake broke the silence with a question. "I wonder if there's any truth to the theory that she was hit on purpose."

The communications were breaking up, but Jenna heard the words theory truth she hit purpose. "What? You're breaking up, Jake."

Jake eased his way through the broken, hanging doorway to the gymnasium as Jenna spoke. He repeated his question.

"Oh, you mean like some secret cargo that someone wanted destroyed?" asked Jenna. "But in 1956, we weren't at war—not a real war."

"Cold war was a war, Jenna. Could have been something as simple as top secret documents or a spy on board."

The findings had the Stockholm's junior officer on the bridge simply making a foolhardy mistake, reading the radar somehow upside down or backwards. The findings never set well with Jake. He had scoured the manifest, every person on board, but even so, a spy would be using an alias, he imagined. Putting these thoughts aside, he checked his dive watch. "We only have twelve minutes left to find Richards. What are you seeing ahead of you, Jen?"

"Parlor room, sitting areas, a bar."

"No floating bodies?"

"None so far, no."

"Be damn sure to check behind the bar. He might've hoped to bring up a bottle or two."

"That'd fetch a pretty penny," she replied.

"He's got to be here somewhere. It's mean a lot to have that donation to the URI Marine Biology Program finalized, and more could come of it, you know."

"I thought the family already made the donation," said Sam from above, listening in on them.

"Not until we have results, Sam, no." Jake realized the gymnasium was a bust.

Sam replied, "My bad assumption."

"Aren't they all bad, Sam?" said Jake. "I'm moving on from here down the length of the corridor other side of the gym, Jenna. I'm getting pretty far in."

"Watch out for hanging wires, pipes, falling debris, you two," Sam warned. "Looks like an explosion hit that area, you're in, Jenna."

"I just found the gash. Huge hole in her side starboard bow. Damn. Looks like Hiroshima."

"Be careful there, sweetheart," warned Sam.

"Just keep capturing this footage, Sam," she told Sam. "Hey, I could escape the ship from here, go up to the top deck and cross back to the strobe lights and guideline."

17

"If you swim out that gash, be damn careful," warned Jake. "That torn metal cuts deep. I got the scar to prove it."

Jenna looked about what was once a state room, one of the many that had been demolished when the Stockholm's reinforced bow plowed into the Andrea Doria, cutting a huge swath of a gash across some forty feet, killing some fifty people at once, washing many of the bodies out to sea as the Stockholm backed its nose out of the wounded ship. One lucky girl wound up inside the Stockholm, unconscious but safe and found hours later in the torn bow. The young woman had been presumed dead for twenty-four hours before she was found unconscious but alive.

Jenna realized she was staring at history, and if this compartment could speak, it would tell one hell of a story. As she moved carefully about the destroyed area, she had to be extra careful. "If Richards came this way, he could easily have gotten tangled in the conduit and wires," she said into her com-link. "And if so, his body could as well be at the bottom of the ship outside, covered over by sand, shell and debris."

"You don't have time to move outside and down her side and dig around, do you?" asked Sam.

"No, she doesn't Sam, and don't encourage her," countered Jake. "Times nearly up for us already."

Jenna stood staring at the enormous gash to her side; something mesmerizing about the gaping hole that looked out on nothing but the sea bottom. It

18

looked as if a bomb had gone off. All the metal was twisted inward, pointing at Jenna like so many ugly giant knife edges. Everywhere building materials, wires, pipes either lay about or hung overhead. What was left of a smashed, twisted bed was forced into a wall, half in, half out of the corridor the other side of the compartment. Jenna imagined a sleeping mother and child in that bed. Of course, she had no idea whose compartment this was, who would have been in that bed, but it was obvious, whoever he or she was, death had instantly found anyone lying there at the time of the impact.

Then she saw something move the stained eaten-away blanket jammed into the destroyed wall and held there as a result. She imagined the dead person beneath this blanket covered in seawater slipping from below the covers, being washed out to sea. Her imagination began to work overtime as the ocean water still played about the blanket, lifting, pulling at it, pushing, tugging in a gentle suggestion to come loose. The little unseen struggle between the blanket and the sea going on for so many years here struck Jenna as poignant. In time the sea always wins, she thought. But this time even so, the blanket would be completely eaten away, the tug of war futile.

She wanted to look away and not give the creepy, undulating blanket another thought; didn't wish to give the deceased in this place another thought. Something in her did want to scour the place, however, for any possible artifacts to take topside with her, anything that could be of value back in the real world. A cup, a piece of china, a wash basin, even one of these ugly pieces of pipe could fetch something in an auction on eBay, and with the camera footage, she could authenticate the object. She'd been disappointed at the bar—no bottles left. Previous divers had gotten to it.

Suddenly, she saw something glinting in her light, something deep in the rubble. A piece of jewelry, she believed.

"Are you watching your time, Jenna?" asked Jake from wherever he'd gotten off to.

"Yeah, yeah," she lied and then glanced at her dive watch. "Shit." She only had eight minutes before she must begin her ascent. Most of that time would be taken up getting back to the guideline.

She moved fast toward the shining object and reached into the pile of rubble that was gently stroked by the seawater that she'd disturbed. She felt the chain and broach at the end of her fingertips. One wrong move, and it would slip from her grasp and fall deeper into the rubble. She slowed her movement and tried to slow her heart rate.

Sam from above was asking questions of her. "Jenna, you're spiking. What is that you're seeing?"

"Piece of jewelry from a passenger. Could be the dive is paid for if I can get…firm…hold…"

"Watch your surroundings, kiddo," Sam cautioned again.

"Not to worry," she assured him just as she brought up the gold chain and diamond-studded broach. She held it up to the camera. It shimmered in the glow of her light. "Fantastic!" she announced.

"Lovely," agreed Sam. "What a find."

"Now get out of there and back to the guideline," said Jake.

"You too," she replied.

"On my way out the way I came. No luck here."

"No sign of Richards here either."

"Next time, we enter elsewhere and take another tack."

"I'll be with you guys then," said Sam. "Three searching is better than two."

"If this broach is real diamonds, maybe we don't need the Richards' family money," Jenna said to the men. "Not that I wouldn't like to help the family out, but maybe some things want to be a mystery so much that we mere mortals ought to let them be."

"You really feel that way, Jenna?" asked Sam, watching her ascend from the ship's gash with ease, going for the lifeline to Explorer II. He then saw Jake caught in her camera, and Sam knew both divers were free of the shipwreck and safely on their way back.

As Jenna and Jake made their way slowly, cautiously up the guideline, at this depth, they had to stop every ten feet to rest and relax their breathing to avoid the bends, a condition that could kill any diver. The risks of bubbles in the blood was compounded greatly during deep dives like this. But slowly, carefully, incrementally, the pair made their way back up, switching over to normal oxygen once they got to a safe level to do so, having weaned off

21

the Trimix. They were soon climbing back onto the deck of the Explorer.

CHAPTER TWO

...whatever we were to
each other that we are still.

The evening on board Explorer II proved calm and beautiful as the sunset had painted the sky over the ocean in deep purple hues. After a meal prepared by Juan Carlos, ship's cook, the team had assembled in the planning room to talk over the next day's dive, and to have a laugh over Jenna's diamonds, which turned out to be a child's costume jewelry. Despite the fact the diamonds were glass, the object had come off the Andrea Doria, which could be proven with a short YouTube video. It still would fetch some funds at an auction just because it was salvaged from the Andrea Doria.

"Some wealthy Italian mogul will love it," joked Dolph Nielsen, a ruddy-complexioned fellow that stood as tall as Jake Stoughton. Dolph spoke with a Norwegian accent and his duties on board were those of chief engineer and technician—to keep everything operating smoothly.

Their chief computer and radar technician on board, Jim Hollande got a good laugh from Jenna's 'diamonds' as he held them up to the light. He then apologized and tried to ease her pain, saying, "To be fair, they did look like diamonds on the feed."

"I've got some more reading to do, folks," said Jake. "Think I am done for the night."

"Dive like that is exhausting," said Sam. "You feel it later, after the adrenaline drop."

Jenna and the others wished Jake a good night, and she agreed about the fatigue. "I am bushed too. Will see you guys bright and early. She was wearing the costume jewelry.

"Don't take it too hard, Jenna," Sam said to her. "I saw a guy once come up with a soggy piece of raisin toast once."

This brought on renewed laughter. Jenna waved it off and disappeared below. At the same time, in his cabin, Jake Stoughton looked over the information that his close friend and one-time dive instructor, Jenna Corey, had forwarded to him long before they had come out here to the Andrea Doria and this joint venture. He recalled her having shouted over the phone, "I just forwarded some old news clippings about the wreck and the dive deaths. It's a wonder, they still allow dives to the Andrea Doria, Jake."

"They won't tell you, sweetheart, but danger is a major part of the allure for divers."

"Yes—the danger rush. I get that, Jake."

"Don't tell anyone," he'd joked.

Jake now stared at the headlines of the various articles that he had lied to Jenna about having read. He felt now that he'd best get to them to cover the lie. She had insisted he read up on the Doria deaths since the ship's demise—the deaths of wreck divers.

One title read: In the Depths, the Andrea Doria Claims Another Diver. A second read: Listing of the Dead Divers at Andrea Doria. Another read: Man

Missing after Andrea Doria Shipwreck Dive. The articles displayed a variety of sources from CNN to the Boston Globe. Some of the articles indicated caches and similar articles. Some were blogs, simple listings of the divers who had died while exploring the shipwreck. Seventeen of them now with Richards' death.

"Jenna, you are a bleeding heart," Jake said after scanning some of the articles. "A sweetheart yourself, but a bleeding heart just the same." Jake knew that to Jenna every premature death during a dive was a tragedy, and Jake agreed, but at the same time diving-related deaths happened all across the globe and at many a shipwreck dive. Still, she was right about one thing. No shipwreck on the bottom of the sea in all of history had claimed as many lives as this one they floated over tonight.

Beyond her degrees and expertise as a diver, Jenna was also a psychic, and she'd had great success working with police departments across the country on active and cold cases. Jake, in a previous life, had been a detective on the Boston Police force. It was there that the two of them had first met. Jenna, on a case which required a black water dive in a real ugly hole called Cheat Lake, had actually guided the divers down into that murky hole. He had watched her go down into the darkness of that lonely lake, a stone's throw from the hanging site of the Salem Witches. She accompanied two police divers to recover a body she was certain beneath the surface. In fact, she had guided them under water and straight to the body.

It was not unusual for her to become a suspect in a murder case herself for this reason, but after working with her on several more cases, and after taking diving instruction from her, Jake had come to respect and admire Dr. Jenna Corey more than any woman or cop that he'd ever known.

In her own state room aboard the Explorer II, Jenna Corey held counsel with herself. She asked herself why she had not shared the eerie feeling she had gotten the moment her hand, gloved as it was, clinched the necklace and broach against her palm. She'd still been bent over the prize, still thinking it authentic diamonds, when she felt the presence behind her, someone staring a hole through her, angry perhaps, or was it more a feeling of jealousy. Angry for taking the bauble from the rubble? Or angry for being in that room on the sunken ship? Or was it jealousy? Jealous of her freedom to leave the ship. Jealous of her corporeal body?

The emotions she had felt when she had taken the chain and broach attached to the necklace had been powerful. Emotions that had so suddenly come over her, welling up from deep within. Possibly it had all to do with the pressure she was under down there. Could've happened to anyone. A feeling that there was some sort of ghostly figure lurking in and around her in that deathtrap of a compartment 250 feet below.

It had been so nebulous a feeling, and nothing that Jenna could define or put her finger on. There had been a sensation but nothing seen. If there was a spirit in that area of the sunken ship, it proved a timid one, possibly a child...possibly the owner of the broach and chain.

"Maybe I should tell the others, or at least Jake. Then again, maybe not." She was having trouble sleeping. It was not terribly late, but she was tired, perhaps overly tired. Too tired to sleep was the common expression for how she felt.

She decided to take a walk on deck. Take a stroll around the ship. Study the last thin line on the horizon. Catch the sound of seagulls overhead. Feel the breeze on her face. To this end, she exited her cabin, looked across at Jake's silent room, and started up. She found the deck and took in all of the sounds and the firm touch of the sea winds on her face and in her wild, red hair. Hair that cascaded with each new sea breeze. She studied the white caps. The sea seemed as restless tonight as Jenna herself. Maybe I disturbed something down there.

But why would a spirit be jealous of her? Not so much jealous of her as jealous of the things she took for granted like the sea, the wind, the stars, the moon, the setting sun, and her ability to interact with life. The feel of vibrations inside her. The feel of her own beating heart. It all got Jenna thinking back to that moment. It hadn't been her imagination. She had felt the tug on her attention. Whoever or whatever it was, this spirit wanted her to linger.

And she might have if Jake and Sam hadn't been in her ear, telling her time's up. The question troubling Jenna now was grim: Did the young girl

27

on board the sunken ship want Jenna's attention or her life? Does this spirit have such power, or am I being foolish? Jenna wondered.

Jacob 'Jake' Stoughton had an old and revered New England family name to protect and honor, but he couldn't just be one of them—one of his dysfunctional family. They had been aghast when he became a policeman and worked his way up to detective, and they never understood his passion for the sea either. His family had been lawyers, judges, and magistrates going back to the founding of Boston. But for Jake, it was stifling—the lot of it. So he had 'disowned' them and followed the beat of his own drummer.

Jacob Henry Stoughton II did research for URI on all diver deaths and compiled data as part of his second job at Woods Hole. It was why Jenna had come to him with the Richards family request of her. Jake and Jenna had in the past spoken about the deaths on the Andrea Doria, and they disagreed about the number of deaths. Jake had it at seventeen, while she had it at twenty-one.

Jenna also believed there were more than either of them knew. She had compiled a list that included rumored information, anecdotal information. His job required exacting figures, and his research data could not confirm her rumored information. Much of that rumored information came in the nature of lurid stories in The Inquirer and other questionable sources.

As a result, Jenna had, after their arguments, sent her articles from the Boston Globe and other 'reliable sources'. Jenna, a noted diving professional for many years, was also a world-renowned authority on diving safety, and for many years now Jake, her student, had surpassed the master. During these same years, Jake's University of Rhode Island second home and office on the Kingston campus was the headquarters for the National Underwater Accident Data Center. This meant that Jake collected and provided information on diving accidents throughout the US, which he folded in with accidents across the globe.

It meant that his research was financed by the National Sea Grant College Program, which in turn meant his center was funded by the National Oceanic and Atmospheric Administration (NOAA) and the U.S. Coast Guard.

Jacob Stoughton received a NOGI in 2002 and in 2014, and he received the U.S. Coast Guard Academy Award for outstanding contributions to the field of diving and marine safety. He was also a recipient of the DEMA Reaching Out Award.

"None of which helps Thom Richards," he told himself now. "You're all Jake, yet two hundred feet below your feet, Thom Richards lost his life diving the Andrea Doria, and you can't find him."

Still, Jake realized that he was not present or the cause of the man's demise or where his body had gotten off to. "There's only so much that people responsible for dive safety can do." But the least he could do was to try as they had today and would tomorrow. And the least he could do right now was to read the information on Richards that Jenna had forwarded ahead of her coming aboard. To this end, despite his weariness, he read the first article which began like a novel:

Two hundred feet below the waves, Thom Richards had work to do.

One of the chains attaching a mooring line to the shipwreck of the Andrea Doria had come loose, a not uncommon occurrence. Thom Richards, 64, had ventured down with two other divers from the dive boat Whahoo to secure the waffling chain. When the job was done, they released a few pieces of foam to rise like jellyfish to the surface. A normal act to signal an all-clear message to those waiting on the surface, many of whom were anxiously awaiting their chance to dive to the Andrea Doria themselves.

Richards, a seasoned scuba diver with the experience and the certification necessary to make the challenging dive to one of the world's most alluring shipwrecks, had a few minutes to explore before he had to ascend. His two companions reportedly 'assumed' he was behind them when they began their ascent. Over an hour and two hundred feet later, they discovered Richards had not surfaced with them.

To surface from two hundred feet took approximately an hour and fifteen minutes. It was a grueling ordeal and many dangers attached to such an ascent, and a man had to care for himself to the degree he had no opportunity to be watching out for others. The first of the three divers Mike Hartzel, arrived at the surface. About 15 minutes later, the next diver, Terry Dunn, surfaced, handing up his gear before climbing onto the stern. He looked around for Richards, the bearded, jovial bartender on the mainland.

Hartzel said, "Hey, where's Thom? He was supposed to come up"

The news went around the dive boat like a brush fire. "Where in hell is he?" asked Garrett Tomlinson, an experienced diver and instructor who paid to make his long-awaited first trip to the Andrea Doria.

Terry Dunn said, "I thought I saw him just below the surface." Dunn immediately leapt back into the water to look for Richards but to no avail. There was no sign of the oldest man on the boat that day except for the captain. Tomlinson prepared to dive in search of Richards, but Captain Risley ordered in no uncertain terms, "No one's playing hero here, sir. I got two divers still down there aside from Richards."

Tomlinson argued for going to search for the body.

"No one's going down to the Doria. My orders are law here."

Instead, the Coast Guard was called. Planes searched from the air, and a cutter trolled the area.

Deep underwater, another diver on the wreck, unaware of the hectic activity above, saw something that seemed strange. A diver had left his strobe light attached to the lifeline attached between the shipwreck and the Whahoo above. It would be an

hour before this lady and her husband could surface
and report on what they'd seen. And what they
hadn't seen.

CHAPTER THREE

...whatever we were to
each other that we are still.

Everyone on board knew some smattering of the history of the Italian luxury liner Andrea Doria and her glory days before she sank in July 1956. Everyone knew the cause of her sinking; how she'd been rammed and fatally wounded by the MS Stockholm in what became an infamous maritime disaster. Of about 1,700 passengers and crew on board, some fifty people were killed.

And the Andrea Doria had been lying on her starboard side on the ocean floor ever since. But no one knew until now that her death toll was far from finished.

In the 59 years since the Doria went down, no less that seventeen wreck divers had died attempting to reach her deck or return from it. Some in this number had gotten lost inside the ship's collapsing compartments or had fallen prey to faulty equipment, and all had run out of time and the air they breathed. A few had almost made it back but had suffered the onslaught of debilitating decompression sickness, also known as the bends. Others had collapsed when their hearts simply gave out—according to autopsies done on the remains. Still others had not been found and were presumed

33

to be entombed in the bowels of the shipwreck, possibly forever.

Regardless of the abnormal number of diving deaths in and around the Andrea Doria, she still enticed divers. The draw to her never slowed, never declined.

Jake thought of the ship resting under about 250 feet of cold, dark, treacherous North Atlantic in an area no one could ever drop his guard against. The ocean like any forest was unforgiving, and apparently wished to protect what she had swallowed.

Jake also knew that the Doria had become one yardstick by which the world's best divers measured themselves. Divers trained for years and spent tens of thousands of dollars on sophisticated equipment and custom gas mixtures that allowed them to plunge far below the limits of recreational scuba divers.

To make extra money, Jake had worked on some of the tour boats that dared bring divers to the Andrea Doria. He'd been on board for some of the early deaths at the dive site as well. He gave a thought to the dead and to those who had dived without incident to and from the shipwreck. Every diver had his own reason for wanting to kneel on the historic hull, and for some that was plenty enough. But others wanted more than that. Others rummage through the wreck in search of mementos — china from the well-appointed cruise liner to take home and frame. And every once in a while, someone gets lucky, he thought. He recalled back in

2013, a pair of divers from Nova Scotia had returned to the surface somehow carrying a 75-pound bell that once adorned the Doria's deck. That baby netted those boys a fortune.

"For me, it was a challenge," said Sam Kent as they all shared a light breakfast in the galley. Sam was a hard-bitten, tough old fellow, likeable and always in good spirits. He worked as a diving safety officer at the New England Aquarium. He had made one dive to the Andrea Doria before now, but only after five years of preparation. "I knew that not everybody could do it," he was telling Juan, their galley cook. Sam had been joking with Carlos that he could take him down to the shipwreck, and Carlos had taken him too seriously, eyes wide, palms sweating and arms waving Sam off. Carlos' Spanish kicked in to say in no uncertain a terms that he was not the kind of fool who wished to go 250 feet below surface to see nothing.

Everyone laughed lightly to see Carlos rush out. "There're many harder wrecks to dive, but the Doria has a cachet all her own," Jenna said to the male divers.

Jake added, "Some of that cachet comes from the wreck's place in history."

Sam shot back, asking, "Is cachet anything like Tar-jeh? Reminds me, I need to pick up a cheap kayak for my nephew."

"Jake's talking about the drama of that 1956 night," explained Jenna.

"Well-chronicled in book and film," continued Jake. "Not that its remoteness doesn't add to her allure."

"Aye on that score," agreed Sam.

They were sixty nautical miles off Nantucket, the Andrea Doria below them, very near the continental shelf, where the ocean plunged sharply deeper. "Although few divers openly acknowledge it," Jake said in a more somber tone, "the danger is for some of us its own draw."

"There's so many things that can go wrong on a dive, any dive, but this place…" Sam pushed back from the galley table.

"And divers who are advanced enough to attempt the Doria are quite aware of every potentiality except the one that takes their lives." Jenna took in a deep breath, her eyes on the list of dead men who'd lost their battle with the infamous shipwreck.

"Few of the hazards are within a diver's control," replied Jake.

"At lease we all acknowledge that fact," said Sam. "Not so much every diver coming out on the tour boats like the John Jack."

"Did you read the articles I sent you, Jake?"

"Sure I did. Interesting but…" he shrugged "not much in the way of details. I mean even down to the men who've died while diving the wreck, few details, such as their training. I brought the list with me to show Sam and Jim here what we've been talking about, you and me." Jake produced several pages, the list of seventeen divers who'd lost their lives to Andrea Doria dives and the scant details around each name. "They're all there. The known ones."

"The known ones?" asked Jim.

"The ones we know about for sure, yes. In chronological order. The deaths began in 1980."

Sam and Jim took an instant interest and both looked over the list which read:

John Barnett, 1980, on board Sea Hunter I, recovery by Stan Smith & Gary Gentile. Barnett found expired lying inside wreck on the promenade deck. Barnett a diver since the early 70's and by many called an accomplished diver. He was getting into shape to dive the Doria and had made a trip on the Wahoo two weeks before his Doria dive. On that trip, John had a problem surfacing behind the boat and needed assistance. A swimmer went in to assist, and when Barnett came aboard the boat he was fatigued and disoriented. He'd panicked, unable to find the anchor line and so he'd made a free swimming ascent (very dangerous). The captain of the Wahoo suggested Barnett not make his Doria dive as he was not in condition to make the extreme dive at that time. Two weeks later, he dived to Doria and never returned, his body found by other divers.

"That's a stark story alright," said Sam.

"Aye, tis and sad," agreed Jim Hollande when Dolph Nielsen came in and asked what they were looking over. He quickly looked over Jake's shoulder. The three men now read on:

Francis Kennedy, July 14, 1984, 37 years old, of Wrentham, MA. Charter boat Wahoo. Kennedy ran out of gas during ascent after making a 230-foot dive inside the wreck he was looking for Artie Kirshner's dropped china bag. down a stair well, his depth gauge read 230FSW. Wahoo, Captain Steve Bielenda again made the grim report.

John Ormsby, Aug. 1, 1985, 27 years old, of Key West, FL. died tangled in wire cables inside Gimbel's hole in the wreck. Ornsby was dive partners with Billy Deans. Young John broke the dive plan with Deans and swam away leaving him. Ormsby entered the China Hole where he became entangled in the hanging cables and became trapped at 210 FSW just under the entrance to the hall to the dining room. Wahoo, Captain Steve Bielenda.

Joe Drozd, July 15, 1988, 42, Stonington, CT. Dive boat Seeker. Diving with two buddies, Joe freaked out became disoriented and would not take assistance; he spat out his regulator and drowned. Seeker.

Matthew G. Lawrence, July 2, 1992, 32, of Miami Lakes, FL. Seeker. Poor dive planning his tanks had inadequate mix for the dive he tried to make, he died 14 minutes into dive at 260 feet trying to recover Rosary beads inside the wreck. Seeker, Captain Bill Nagel.

Michael William Scofiled, July 15, 1992, 36, of Soquel, Calif. Seeker, Captain Bill Nagel

Robert Santulli, July 12, 1993, 33, Port Jefferson. Coast Guard investigation found he had panicked after becoming disoriented inside wreck at depth of 210 feet, he struggled with his dive buddy Peter Haralobotas, being narced and in distress, during the struggle his regulator fell out of his mouth and he drowned. Sea Hunter III, Captain Sal Arena.

Craig Sicola, 1998, Seeker, Captain Dan Crowell

Richard Roost aka Scuba God, Seeker, Captain Dan Crowell

Vincent Napoliello died diving on Andrea Doria. Seeker, Captain Dan Crowell

Charles J. McGurr, 1999, died of apparent heart attack preparing for a second dive from Seeker, Capt. Crowell. Coast Guard report.

Christopher Murley, 1999. Drowned on the surface. Seeker, Captain again Dan Crowell, owner, John Moyer & Steve Nagiewicz. Official cause of death: The medical examiner listed the official cause of death as drowning. At some point while Chris Murley was being towed/pushed toward the stern. Became unconscious, causing him to lose control of his neck muscles and his face fell into the water. What caused him to lose consciousness is not known, however, the combination of his moderate arteriosclerotic heart disease, diabetes, obesity and hypertension may have contributed. Cardiomegaly, which is an enlargement of the heart, can also not be ruled out as a contributing factor.

William Schmoldt, 2002. Died from rapid ascent to the surface/decompression sickness. Aboard John JJack, captain/owner Joseph Terzuoli of Wall, N.J.

David Bright, 2006. Researcher. Died from decompression sickness.

Terry DeWolf, 2008, of Houston, TX, died during dive on wreck, cause of death undetermined. John JJack, captain/owner Joseph Terzuoli of Wall, N.J.

Michael LaPrade, 2011, of Los Angeles, CA died during a dive on the wreck. John Jack, Captain Rich Benevento

After Sam and Jim familiarized themselves with the list, Sam said, "Last two aren't on the list. Fella who died in 2015 and this fellow you two are searching for."

"List is incomplete," admitted Jenna. It does need updating."

Jake added, "And there's a lot to be desired as it is. Some dates missing, ages, other details."

"But it does give you some idea of the scope...the size of this problem," she said, eye-balling Sam.

"You don't have to start worrying about me, Jenna. I am in fine shape, just fine, and I've made the dive before."

"We all agreed that everyone should be fully informed before going to Doria, Sharky," said Jake.

"That's all this is, Sam, and just how did you get that nickname? Sharky?"

"Oh, hell...picked that up when I was a snot-nosed junior high kid at the YMCA. I was the only one in my group to move up from minnow to Shark. Some friends started calling me Sharky, and it stuck."

"I compiled this list for general information," she explained to Sam. "Much of it is from stories told by those present. Memories aren't always too reliable. I've tried to get all the Coast Guard reports, but some of them are sketchy at best as well. I've spent a lot of time with Jake because he, too, had collected a lot of information."

The men listened to her attentively. Jenna was an attractive woman and brilliant as well as a superb diver. She said now, "To understand deep diving and make these kinds of dives, you should have extensive deep diving experience, be physically and psychologically ready for the dive."

"Jenna believes that many of those seventeen who've died here, that they were undergoing either depression or some form of mental disorder, and hey, it makes sense. You go down that deep, and you are already wonky...well hell anything can happen. She believes some of these deaths are attributable to something I'm calling 'suicide by shipwreck'."

"Really? Now that is something to contemplate," replied Dolph, with a shake of his blonde head.

Jim bit his lower lip and shook his head. "Hard thing to prove. Do the families have anything to say about the victim's state of mind?"

"Some do, some do not. Some will not hear of it." Jenna frowned. "Such a stigma still attaches to it. Besides, there's always the insurance policy to take into account."

"I get it," replied Sam.

"Suicide may be painless, but not to those left behind," said Jake.

"Aside from the mental state of the diver, his physical state has to be up on par with the Navy Seal, Olympic competitor or damn close."

"Not to mention the right equipment just for this dive," Jake said.

"And you should have months of experience on all the specialized equipment and being comfortable in the equipment, and breathing the Trimix."

Sam nodded. "I agree. A deep depth diver has to be very familiar with the equipment. I tell my buddies the same. Try it on at home, use it in a pool, a lake, or a spring, and on all dives proceeding a trip to a place like this, shit."

Jim said, "We had a guy out once who couldn't even function in close quarters. Couldn't take the banging around on the boat. I mean it was rough seas, but shit."

"Did he take the plunge sea sick?"

"By then said he was just feeling 'beat up'."

"So did your captain tell him no to the dive?" she asked.

"Of course not," replied Jim. "Customer's always right."

She sighed heavily. Jake said, "Captain of a dive tour has to walk a fine line. Saying to a paying customer to sit this one out doesn't work anyway."

"Too easy for the guy to go along with someone else's dive plan and dive when ready or not," added Dolph, shrugging.

"Dolph's right about that. I've seen it hundreds of times. Far too many risks are taken in our business. First timers in the ocean taken beyond the barrier as a joke, for instance. Good way to get people killed."

"But these men who died diving the Doria," argued Jenna, "they were all well-equipped and had a lot of experience for the most part. If this works out as I expect, this is just episode one. I intend to go ghost hunting on other wrecks. Turn this documentary into a weekly program for TLC."

CHAPTER FOUR

Call me by my old familiar name;
speak to me in the easy way
which you always used.

The dive boat and the captain and crew were very important on tour dives, and the experienced crew were trained to spot nervousness, jitters, drinking, drugs, and other reasons to refuse a man to dive at any depth, much less 250 feet. Those on board such excursions in general understood the captain's word was law, and the crew carried out the captain's wishes. The dive boat captains, in general, were experienced and knowledgeable. Those who ignored their orders or their advice for that matter, often paid a dear price. One thing they insisted on was a written dive plan, and an explanation of how the diver meant to perform in the event of an emergency.

The research vessel, Explorer II, was no different. Sam was acting captain today, and he took the job seriously. All divers, including himself, had to turn in a dive plan with their intentions, the path they planned to pursue, and a plan to return safely along with the plan in case of emergency. The steps to take; the protocol. "If we know where you are, should you need assistance, we know where to find you. If we do not know where you are in that gigantic ship, how then can we assist you?"

Jake and Jenna nodded at all Sam's precautions. Being in the business of dive safety themselves, it was tedious but they knew it necessary as well. As they geared up for the dive now, Sam told them, "I was on the Wahoo in 1985 when the first time in history we used surface supplied oxygen for in water decompression."

"You were with Captain Billy Deans from Key West Divers in 1985?" asked Jenna. "That had to be cool."

"Cool was the 90's with the advent of technical diving, when divers began replacing experience with mixed gases Trimix and Rebreathers. Frankly, I believe these advances—"

"May have contributed to the increase in diver deaths, I'm sure," she finished for him, agreeing.

Christopher Murley on your list of the dead is the perfect example," said Sam. "He was well over his optimum weight, had health issues, and lacked the experience to make extreme dives like the Doria."

"But the equipment gave him all the courage he needed, I'm sure."

Sam nodded, "And in his rush to be certified as a mix-gas advanced Trimix diver, he did it backwards."

"I heard it was all due to the charter boat rules," said Jake, who was ahead of the others in having suited up. "That since he knew the minimum certification required was mix gas "Trimix" certification, Murley was doing his final check out dives on the Doria of all places!"

"That's right. He was not yet certified." Jenna grunted, hefting her tanks.

Sam helped Jenna with her tanks. "That's what I read in the Coast Guard report."

"Murley was nowhere near qualified to make deep dives, especially not only on the Doria. Part of the problem was he was one of two paying customers on the trip, and if Murley didn't pay, the trip would not have happened."

"As I recall, Murley drowned on the surface while being assisted up."

"Yeah, I read the report too," said Jenna. "Including the written reports of every person aboard the Seeker."

It was a pursuit nearly as old as the infamous shipwreck itself. Divers first plunged into the waters off Nantucket, Massachusetts, to catch a glimpse of the Andrea Doria only a day after the ship sank in July 1956. That first dive netted photos for Life magazine. A spread that literally spread word that she could be reached by truly experienced divers. Later, another expedition led to a documentary about the deadly collision that had killed more than 50 people when the Italian luxury liner collided with another ship. So for decades, the site became increasingly popular with the most daring divers until it was coined as the 'Mount Everest' of wreck diving.

Officials continued to warn of its dangers. It proved dangerous just to get to the shipwreck site, 240 feet underwater at its highest end. In the past decade alone, seven men who'd set out to reach the wreck never returned. Both Jenna and Jake knew there were likely others who'd died during unreported dives as there were unscrupulous boat men who were paid handsomely to ignore the rules. Most of these were night dives over Andrea Doria.

"Another diver went missing this week and is presumed dead," said Jake.

"Oh no," groaned Jenna.

"Coast Guard said it suspended the search for the missing 56-year-old man Wednesday night. Notified his next of kin."

"Came over the radio," shouted Jim from above. "The diver was last heard from on Tuesday while diving the wreck." Hollande had to shout over the sound of the spray. The waves had begun to shiver the research vessel, tossing them about. Jim added, "Another diver reported having been with the guy underwater, but didn't see him when he got back to the surface."

"Sound familiar?" asked Jenna.

"The Coast Guard crews, by air and by sea, searched more than 350 square nautical miles over 30 hours as they looked for a sign of the missing diver before announcing the search had been called off.

It was a difficult decision, I'm sure. They vacated just ahead of our arrival." Jim seemed to relish being the man with all the answers. "Taped it for you guys! I'll put it on the speakers." Hollande did so, and after an initial report, a Mark Gannon, Chief of Response at the Coast Guard came on. Jake knew the man well as he was in charge of Sector

47

Southeastern New England. He said, "Our primary goal, those of us who serve the Guard, is to rescue those in need and to save lives. So it is extremely disheartening and crushing to us as it is for the families of those lost at sea anytime we are unable to accomplish our goal."

Gannon's remarks were followed by a female voice. "The shipwreck site is a popular destination for advanced divers and charter services that bring people to the area." She identified herself as Lt. Karen Cross, Coast Guard spokeswoman, "But given how deep it is," she said, "it's not an appropriate spot for recreational divers."

The risky underwater trek to this particular shipwreck had become so notorious that it was the topic of a 2002 book entitled Deep Descent: Adventure and Death Diving the Andrea Doria. Author Kevin F. McMurray explained the ship's mystique, how it enticed people into the depths of the Atlantic: "Her untimely demise, the tragic loss of life, the rescue of her survivors by her heroic brethren, and of course the whims of the open oceans that brought about her destruction."

"Why risk it?" divers were constantly asked.

Sam, Jake, and Jenna understood why. As divers who remembered or had studied the ship's dramatic story, the sinking, how pristine she looked even under water, there was a yearning to touch her deck, to wander her corridors and staterooms, to see the ballroom, the gymnasium, the shops, the sitting rooms and cigar lounges, not to mention the captain's quarters and the bridge. There was a yearning to bring home a piece of her, to discover something within her that told a personal story and that could bring a high price—if a man could part with it. An artifact from the Andrea Doria to preserve, display, share with a maritime museum, and profit from, not to mention the cachet of being the one who returned from inside Doria with that relic.

The Coast Guard officials offered more words of warning in their statement on this week's missing diver. "The ocean is unforgiving," the statement said. "The Coast Guard reminds everyone on the water, whether diving, snorkeling, boating or swimming to stay vigilant, especially in unfamiliar places."

"So how're you feeling, Sam?" asked Jenna. "Are you sure you're over that queasiness you were complaining about yesterday?"

"You are well enough to join Jen and me, right, Sharky?" asked Jake.

"All suited up and can't be talked out of it."

"You call that an answer?" asked Jenna.

"I'm fine! Fit as a fiddle and anxious as a shark to get moving."

"Then we'd all best get moving," said Jake. "See if we have better luck today finding Richards' body."

"Wish we could raise the entire ship," said Jenna. "Put it on display in Boston or at Woods Hole."

"Dreamer! That would cost a fortune. You'd have to do Warren Buffet to accomplish that, Jen."

"You and Warren would have to get all the bodies out of her before you put her on display, Jen," added Sam who shared a belly laugh with Jake and Jim, how overheard this.

"Hey, Jim, did you catch the name of the latest victim of the Doria?" shouted Jenna up to the young technician who'd be monitoring their progress below via screens in the operations room.

"Evans, no-no, Evan Hindmon. Why?"

"In case we run into him to say hello. Then she whispered to Jake, "Wonder if his family's going to put up a reward."

"What are we now, Jen? Bounty hunters?"

"Today, we're body hunters—Richards. If we happen on this new guy," she shrugged. "We'll see."

"Make for good footage for your documentary, you mean?"

"Of course it would make for great TV. The idea is to make money for our shared passion, right?"

"Right...sure."

"I'm in lead, gents," she said and dropped over the side back first. Sam followed with Jake coming up the rear. They had agreed upon their dive plan that Sam would be between them, but Jake was supposed to have taken the lead. Jenna was showboating.

CHAPTER FIVE

*Let my name be ever the household
word that it always was. Let it be spoken
without effect, without the ghost of a
shadow on it.*

Thom Richards had taken up diving late in life, aiming only to have some fun during a Cancun vacation in 1991. He'd told Sam Kent that after he got the bug, he dived in Australia to—as he'd put it: "See the Great Barrier Reef before she completely died off." That had been in 2001.

In news accounts later of his mysterious death and unfound remains, family members said he purely loved his newfound pleasure, and that at very least, he died doing what he loved.

As he advanced through recreational diving and into what's known as technical diving, Richards had vigorously pursued more challenging goals, traveling the Eastern Seaboard and eventually visiting the Doria several times without incident. But Thom, who was a retired high school English teacher at Woodrow Wilson High in Beckley, West Virginia, a land-locked state, was not one to push the envelope too far, and he could certainly not be called a reckless man or tagged as a daredevil.

"He wasn't chasing the danger of the Doria or anything like that," Sam had confided to Jim Hollande. "He was very conscious of the safety risks. He was meticulous about his equipment and his gear."

Topside, Jim Hollande watched the monitors, paying particular attention to the vital signs of his friend and mentor, Sharky. Sam Kent, with about 3,000 dives under his belt, had a reputation for careful preparation and attention to detail. Two days before, Sam and a diving buddy drove down to southern tip of Rhode Island, where the John Jack had been chartered by Sharky's side job, Underwater Expeditions, a Rhode Island-based diving outfit. Richards, the fellow that Sharky, Jake and Jen were so anxious to find today, had been on board as part of the John Jack's crew, intending to work and dive on back-to-back Doria trips.

Sharky had kept this fact from Jake and Jenna and had made Jim Hollande promise to keep it between them. He felt some guilt over Richards' death. He had told Jim that on Monday, after the rocky overnight run to the Doria site, this guy Richards wasn't feeling up to the challenging night dive.

"He wasn't feeling 100 percent," said Sam, one of more than a dozen divers, including crew, on the John Jack that day. "I don't think he'd had enough sleep."

So Richards, patient and cautious, helped others ready their equipment and seal up their suits. Sam had put him to work. "He was a nice old fella, really," Sam had told Jim. "By Tuesday morning, Richards seemed to have found his sea legs. Hell, we traded stories over breakfast." Hollande could tell that Sharky had been immediately fond of the easy-going older diver with the white beard and sharp wit.

"Jim, it was my fault," said Sharky.

"How can you say that, Sam?"

"He took on a task that I should have seen to. When the mooring line tethering the John Jack to the Andrea Doria needed to be rescued, Richards jumped to it...suited up. By this time, I had learned he'd had 1000 dives under his belt, and he had good, sophisticated equipment..."

Hearing this, Jim had pictured deep water diving apparatus. Rebreather on his back; a dry suit covering his body; heavy, bulbous tanks filled with the various compressed gasses strapped to his back and under his arms. And yet it was the last time Thom Richards dropped below the waves.

Jim told himself he shouldn't worry about Sharky and the others. They were all three skilled divers, and for Sharky, the journey down to the Andrea Doria was a fairly simple deal. After splashing into the water, he'd have held onto the mooring line attached to the wreck below and simply allowed himself to sink. That poor dead guy down there, Richards, he hadn't had a line to guide him down. For all anyone knew, he was caught in a powerful current, snatched away, and off the coast of Africa somewhere by now.

When it was discovered that Richards was missing, there really was no telling where he'd got off to. Sharky said he had dived in to examine the stern of the shipwreck, but that his attempt was not reported in any Coast Guard documents, and he wanted it that way then and he wanted it to remain so. Jim tried to reassure him that he couldn't carry such guilt around, but Sharky was Sharky. He felt responsible. "That should have been me; it was my job, not his."

Jake experienced the descent downward to the Andrea Doria in his every fiber. He loved diving; it was in his blood, his DNA. But right now the dive felt both routine and wary at once. Save for minor adjustments to his rebreather, there truly was little to do on the roughly four-minute journey down. At about 200 feet below the surface, the amount of oxygen in the air humans breathed on land became toxic under this pressure. The rebreather controls made it an easy matter for the three divers to switch to a gas mixture that wouldn't knock them out, or send them into convulsions. The controls were now substituting some of the oxygen and nitrogen in air for another inert gas — helium. The resulting mix of three gases divers called Trimix, both a brand name and a generic term nowadays.

Water that's greenish near the surface darkens and then turns gray. At the bottom, it's nearly black, and the hulking wreck looms in the dark. Alighting on hands and knees, divers greet the Doria on all fours.

But for all the preparation and advanced equipment, divers had only a few minutes to explore the Doria. The more time divers spent breathing the specially tailored mix of gases required to survive at such depths, the longer they'd have to spend making their way back to the surface. A typical Doria dive involved only fifteen or sixteen minutes exploring the wreck before the three divers had to leave the ship behind or face death.

During those few minutes now, Jenna, Sam, and then Jake affixed strobe lights to the mooring line to help find their way back. Some hook lines of their own, wound into reels on their equipment, onto the wreck near the mooring line so they could more easily find their way back when their time in the wreck would run out.

All three of them were well aware that some of those who had died got tangled in wires and debris, while others simply got lost inside the wreck. Others appeared to have panicked, spit out their mouthpieces and drowned. But most of those now dead had actually make their way back to the mooring to start their long, slow ascent, dying along the way. Typically of either the bends or a heart attack. Some were seen rushing madly to the surface, throwing all caution to the wind—and killing themselves in the bargain.

Jake was well aware that every minute at the bottom dramatically increased decompression time. For a dive of typical duration, the return to the surface required about an hour, with stops nearly every 10 feet, pausing for precisely timed intervals. Little wonder the panicked diver got himself—and often others—killed on ascent more often than descent.

The gases inhaled and absorbed at the pressurized environment far below the surface bubbled in a diver's blood like the soda inside a tin can when the pressure around a man began to decrease on ascent. The stops allowed time for the body to acclimate, off-gassing the helium and nitrogen safely while breathing in an increasingly oxygen-rich mix.

Foot by foot, divers must slowly make their way toward the surface, lightly gripping the line, and keeping one's patience and a consistent depth in the water can be arduous and draining. The current can be strong, and the boat's bobbing moves the line, ripping it across palms, tearing through gloves as divers wait out each decompression stop. But for now they were on the deck of the Andrea Doria, and all such concerns faded in the excitement of the moment.

For Sam 'Sharky' Kent, however, his thoughts were on board another deck, the deck of the old John Jack. His thoughts during the descent had returned him to the moment when Richards had insisted on doing the work below, taking that tether down to the shipwreck.

Then came the stomach lurching moment when Richards failed to come up. Another diver said he was sure that Richards was behind him at or around the twenty-foot decompression stop, which if true would have meant that Thom Richards was almost back to the John Jack when last seen. The other diver said he'd watched as Richards signaled to him, and that he'd signaled back and then headed up to the boat. This fellow had said Richards looked as calm as any man in the water ever might, waving as if standing at a school bus stop, was how the fellow had put it.

That's when Sam had frantically put his suit on and grabbed all his gear and plunged into the water to look for his newfound friend below the boat. But when there was no sign of Thom, Captain Crowell, who'd given the order that no one follow Sam's example, radioed the Coast Guard.

The captain then shouted for everyone to start throwing beer cans and garbage overboard to track the current, giving the Coast Guard rescue crews a trail to follow in case Richards had been ripped from the tether line and was taken off by the sea. Meanwhile, Sam Sharky Kent was by then uselessly bobbing on the surface. Within about five minutes, a Coast Guard plane was overhead.

"Visibility's at least a mile," Captain Crowell shouted out to Sam. "If he had surfaced behind the boat, we'd have seen him by now, Sam! Get back here."

Sam instead dove for the shipwreck, allowing for the other diver who claimed to have seen Richards wrong. Down at the Doria, the handful of remaining divers were unaware of the chaos overhead. The last two divers approached the line to retrieve their strobe lights and saw a third strobe affixed to the line. When Sam came down, they pointed to the strobe light, confused by its still being there.

Sam read the letters on the strobe light, the initials TP—Thom's initials. By this time, Sam knew that Thom was gone. Wherever he was, he was no longer breathing. Still not wishing to give up without a fight, Sam explored a section of the ship closest to Thom's strobe light, hoping against hope that at very least, he might find the man's remains and get the body to the surface.

But he only got so far. He felt a pressure growing against his chest, and he feared his own panic attack coming on. He got nervous. He thought he saw something unusual, a young lady's lacey dress and hat, a bonnet of sorts, all undulating in the water, and when the hat turned, he realized it was atop a head, and when the hallucination turned fully around, there she was, a young girl all dressed to go to the dance or some ball. Her eyes like water, her expression changing with the light from a wide smile to a horrible scream, and then she was gone as suddenly as she had appeared.

Sam realized something was wrong in his head, the mix gases, the pressure, and with his time running low, he turned and rushed back to the lifeline to make his slow, shaky ascent. Feeling like a fool, having accomplished nothing, fearful now for his own life, he fell back on his training. He must go up and up at the orderly, slow ascent that would keep him alive. Anything else meant sure death. But what the hell did I see, he still wondered, and he still had no idea if it had all been in his head or if he had seen a ghost on the Andrea Doria.

When he'd gotten back on the John Jack, asking if there was any news and learning that there was none, it was an hour and fifteen minutes later. Sam reported seeing Thom's strobe light at the wreck. "He's somewhere inside that ship. He'd have come up with his strobe light otherwise."

The other diver shouted back at this, saying, "I tell you, he was right behind me on the line!"

"You were mistaken then of what you saw," Sam shouted back, his fists clenched, prepared to fight, all his rage and anger boiling to the surface when the captain stepped in and broke it up.

"Richards never left the Doria," Sam said for them all to hear. "Being on a rebreather, he could have been alive, caught on or in something…wiring, a net, a slammed door."

"Perhaps we should go down and search for the man," said one of the divers on board.

"We'll have none of this hero shit," the captain firmly said. "Hear me, all of you. We've lost a man, and that's tragic, terribly tragic, but this is my boat, and I won't be losing anymore to the Andrea Doria, not today. We leave it to the professionals now." He pointed using his pipe to the overhead helicopter and the cutter that had arrived earlier. "As for us, gentlemen, we're heading home so you can all have dinner and wine with a loved one."

It had taken days for Sam to finally come to the conclusion that Captain Crowell had been prudent and wise that evening. Three other divers wanted to go down after Sam had returned. They showed guts in the wanting. But the captain had their gear

59

stowed away, prohibiting anyone from doing what he called a 'Clutch Cargo' dive, adding, "If Sharky here could do nothing for Richards, none of you can. You'd just cause more bad publicity for the sport you love. So settle down."

Later, other experienced divers and Coast Guard officials said the decision to keep everyone aboard the Jack Johns, while a difficult call for the captain, was the right call and the wise one.

When Sam had shared all this with old friend Jake, he'd told him everything except for the guilt he felt, and except for the apparition he 'thought' he'd witnessed inside the Doria.

Jake had replied, "I'm glad I wasn't the decision-maker on that boat."

"Me too, Jake. Me too."

"At the same time, if I'd been on that boat at the time, I'd have wanted to do exactly what you did, my friend."

If Richards had ascended without his strobe light and had gotten to the twenty-foot mark below the boat, then his body could have been carried hundreds of yards away as it sank.

Richie Kohler, a wreck diver and shipwreck historian who has led his own Doria expeditions on the *John Jack*, said Pritchards' fellow crew members owed it to him to search.

Everyone had heard of Kohler's own lost diver at the Doria. When a diver was lost near the surface, Kohler had triangulated his position by gauging the current and searched the ocean floor until he found the deceased diver, who'd died of a heart attack.

But that kind of heroics, even Kohler had to acknowledge, might not always be possible. More often than not, location, weather conditions, and equipment played a part. When Pritchards disappeared, the *John Jack's* ladder had broken off while the boat was tooling around the dive site in rough seas, and an aluminum ladder had been attached to the diving platform, making boarding the boat tricky at best. Risking additional divers to search for the lost one may have been the best of a bad situation.

Still, Kohler, Jake, and Sharky had all asked to tag along on the John Jack's next trip to the Doria to search for Pritchards' body but were rebuffed. Sam, who'd been on the Doria at least 100 times, had a problem with that. He'd told Jake and Kohler, "You can at least do some kind of diligence to bring him home."

A couple hours after Pritchards vanished, the *John Jack* left the scene a day ahead of schedule and headed back for port in Nantucket. And about 40 hours after the Coast Guard had arrived, the search was called off. If Pritchards ever surfaced, nobody ever saw him.

The dive team today from Explorer two all knew one thing for certain. What precisely happened to Pritchards and where his remains lay might never be known.

Whether it had been a failure of the man or a failure of the equipment, a medical emergency that might have incapacitated him inside the wreck, or if one of those big swells had brought the *John Jack's* hull down on his head — or something else entirely — the array of possibilities seemed countless, and the mystery as vast as the sea itself.

And Pritchards, with all his experience, had to be well aware of the fact that the ocean loved taking things like ships and lives. He was very well aware of it. Every serious diver was well aware of it, and Pritchards, regardless of having gotten himself killed, knew what he was doing."

Sam had cautioned Jenna and Jake earlier about the possibility they would not find Pritchards. "If he did ascend near the John Jack, his body may eventually emerge in a fishing boat's net, maybe."

Jenna didn't want this for her film. She wanted something far more dramatic. She'd remained silent, while Jake had said, "If he never left the Doria, we may find him, if we get lucky, and if not us, some other diver may one day discover him on another expedition."

"You two are far too grim and skeptical," Jenna finally said. "We are going to find Thom Pritchards' remains."

But even now as they separated, each taking a separate section of the shipwreck cruise liner, just as the dive plan ordered, one thing was certain—the searchers could easily find skeletal remains from long dead, undiscovered previous divers to the wreck, and for now, somewhere inside the Andrea Doria, if not near the shipwreck, Thom Pritchards' corpse was entombed below the waves.

CHAPTER SIX

*Life means all that it ever
meant. It is the same as it ever was, there
is absolutely unbroken continuity.*

Like the Empress of Ireland, the huge Andrea
Doria lay within reach of serious divers, but it was
no place for the faint of heart or untrained or
unprepared. The ship lay perfectly still on her side
like a toy knocked aside by a child's foot. Pristine
save for areas where the ocean life had begun to
take over. The divers of Explorer II now used the
metal handholds along the wounded vessel to pull
themselves along and to speed up their descent to
the entry points each had carefully chosen and
marked out on the diagrams of each deck. Each of
the divers had a separate destination, and the
deepest one had gone to Sam, who'd fought for it
tooth and nail.

Topside, on the war room console, Jim
Hollande had a copy of the diagram of the ship's
decks, red-penciled with each diver's dive plan. It
all looked so easy on paper, like marking one of
those labyrinths found in a child's coloring book,
but once inside the ship with the darkness and the
murky waters and silt, a diver could fast become
disoriented and turned around and eventually
trapped. For this reason, as each diver moved along
their chosen path, a strobe light was magnetically

attached, creating a lighted way out the way the diver had come, a way home again to the lifeline.

The dead ship lay on its port side, the huge gash in her buried in the sand. To get to that area, a diver had to go from starboard promenade, down several flights to the lower deck, cross to the port side and travel the crushed corridors there. No easy task, but Jenna insisted she had to return to that stateroom area where she'd found the costume jewelry, claiming there was something alluring about the crash site where Stockholm had rammed Doria. She had not gotten to the other side of the gash and something told her that Pritchards' body might well be in the next ruined compartment over from the one she'd made it to. She'd be faster getting in and out this time as she knew the way.

All three of the men cautioned her against going too far and taking one too many risks. Jim Hollande had called it the 'bridge too far' syndrome. Jenna scoffed and insisted she knew what she was doing.

Jake Stoughton by comparison wanted to get to the ball room where the captain and crew would be patiently dancing with elderly passengers, entertaining as it were at the last set the band would have been playing. Band equipment along with tables and chair had fallen over and moved as if granted life as the ship immediately listed to port. She never regained an upright position but slowly, over eleven hours listed more and more to port until completely on her side, kissing the sea.

64

"Why the ballroom? It's been a place of heavy traffic since divers have dived her?" asked Sam.

"It's a large vacuum in a sense. Pritchards' body could have been caught up elsewhere but that area with so many doors on so many sides…well, it sucks in and out like the lungs of the shipwreck, still breathing. I know it's been searched once by previous divers, but it's time we put eyes on it again."

The reasoning seemed logical to Jim Hollande as he monitored the movements of the divers and their vital signs. Meanwhile, Sam had selected the kitchen area. "I want to inspect the pantries," he'd joked. "For a good cognac." Then he had spoken seriously, saying, "Pritchards told me when I talked to him once that he believed there might be something of value in the walk-in freezer. What it was, I have no clue, but suppose he was fixated on that spot, actually went into the freezer and got locked in?"

"Interesting theory," Jake had replied and Jenna had nodded. "Anything's possible," Sam had added.

"But what do you think Pritchards meant about something being in the freezer?"

"He joked that it could be the frozen body of Mussolini or a mummy bound for a museum in the states."

"Very funny," Jenna had replied, adding a mocking laugh."

"Cryogenics he'd said, but then he laughed. "Frosty, ha! Like you are now, Jenna."

"That's hardly nice, Jake."

Jim Hollande had listened in on the crazy conversation but had remained silent despite grimacing here and there. He now saw that each of the divers had gone into different areas of the ship. He worried most about Sam's choice as it was a complicated matter getting to the kitchen area and the wall of freezers. There were four walk-in freezers. Which one, if any held a prize? Pritchards' body or Mussolini's? Or the mummy or all three? Hollande held back a laugh at the notion. He tried to shake off his gnawing worries for all three of the living divers at the moment inside Andrea Doria.

The seabed at the shipwreck was unpredictable at best. It was in an area where underwater weather conditions could and did change suddenly and drastically. It often went from clear and calm to a ripping current filled with enough sediment to create a blinding fog.

Then you had your man-made dangers. Fishing nets draped the hull, but even more dangerous than nets and the whim of the currents, were the treacherous, invisible web of tough monofilament fishing line. Fins, tanks, limbs were easily caught in lost, errant lines of it. And then there were the sharks, and on rarer occasions, giant squid.

On three separate screens, Jim watched each diver's progress inside the chilling, dark rooms and corridors that formed the dead ship's interior, places where previous divers had become hopelessly lost. Still, the rewards for a diver to venture to the Andrea Doria, coming this deep, to rediscover a ship as yet recognizable as the wondrous luxury liner of her day, a ship that daily cruised the southern Atlantic route in the 1950s, was fulfilling on many levels. Such a well of accomplishment for a deep sea diver that the danger and risks were not an issue.

Much of the deck hardware and all three swimming pools remained clearly visible, and lifeboat davits still jutted from the boat deck, and great cranes dominated her bow. The ship's name across her bow and stern could still be read.

On a calm and bright day like the one Jenna, Sam, and Jake had found today, the visibility great, a diver could swim fairly easily along the portside promenade deck, where a person's eyes would be attracted to the luminous green 'sky' of the sea overhead. And how strange it always felt to watch the giant propeller reveal itself in slow fashion as a diver neared the stern, where a myriad of colored coral reflected back from the great, bronze port propeller looming above the sea floor as if levitating. With each dive to the Doria, the enormous propeller seemed to enlarge her dimensions quite on her own, without the help of human hands.

That same enormous propeller always cautiously revealed itself, due in part to the angle of the divers' descent but also the encrusted coral and unattached sea life nestling in and among the blades. Nature's own camouflage.

"That propeller gets me every time," Sam had said to the others before they'd left the deck of

Explorer II. "You know, how it seems to magically appear…to loom out of the underwater darkness."

Many divers to this Wreck ventured inside through 'Gimbel's Hole', a wide opening cut by Peter Gimbel years before. Gimbel had cut the large hole in order to retrieve the ship's safe. Once inside the Andrea Doria, a diver could visit the dining room, or the gift shop, the gym, a stateroom or two, some corridors. Most anywhere a diver could get into and out of safely, that room was left stripped of any artifacts or valuables. Emptied of anything worthy of salvaging.

The way it shook out, after twenty minutes from tether line to shipwreck and back, twenty minutes proved maximum in actual time exploring the wreck, fifteen to be prudent. After the fifteen or twenty minutes that a diver had inside, he had a good ninety minutes returning to the surface; ninety minutes decompressing or else his head explodes. Ninety long minutes before his head could come above water. To laymen, non-divers, it always sounded foolish to go so far and have so little time at the site. But the diver brought back with him or her unforgettable images of ruined beauty, ruined luxury, and the end of an era in ocean travel.

The team of three searching for Pritchards' remains had synchronized their watches, and had all agreed to be back at the tether precisely on time. Any other action put them all in danger for their lives. No matter what they encountered inside the shipwreck, their first duty was to stay alive. And because the time was so limited, and the stakes so

68

high, that Sharky thought Jake was wrong in his choice of areas to search. In Sam's estimation, there was no need to repeat looking in areas they'd already investigated. It was highly unlikely that Pritchards' body was floating freely around the now haunted ship—haunted by the dead divers that she had claimed.

All three of the divers knew the ship's history well. It was at a time when the postwar passenger boom was at its peak. More than fifty passenger liners sailed the sea lanes between Europe and America. Among the most splendid, two new ships of the Italian Line, the Cristoforo Colombo and the Andrea Doria. Both had been built for luxury travel, not speed. They took full advantage of the sunnier southern route. The Doria had graceful lines, the public rooms were lavishly decorated and filled with artwork, and her first-class suites proved the most rarified as any that had come before her, including the Titanic. She was the first liner to sport three outdoor swimming pools along with one interior pool. She was the best the times had to offer, the pride of Italy, a ship combining 1950s modernity and Italy's extraordinary artistic heritage.

She'd been well-contoured, built to work, and outfitted with state-of-the-art navigational equipment, including two sets of radar—the still developing technology that'd transformed maritime battlefields on the high seas and was now standard equipment on such a vessel. But should the radar fail and somehow a collision happen, the Andrea

Doria was—in theory—unsinkable. Still, that had been said of the Titanic.

Owners called it unsinkable to sell tickets, of course, but her eleven watertight compartments had been constructed so as to keep her afloat even if any two compartments were breached. Anything safer than that, not even the greatest skeptic could imagine. Her builders said she would never list more than fifteen degrees, ever. As an additional safety measure, her lifeboats could still be launched at a twenty-degree list to either side. Despite it all, the ship became the last great transatlantic passenger liner destined to be lost before that magical era faded away.

The Doria story provided vivid evidence that despite all the safety gadgets, the mind of man is fallible. The same equally applied following the loss of the Titanic, the Empress of Ireland, and countless ships claimed by the sea.

Human frailty in cahoots with bad luck, Jake thought now. Such thoughts made the collision and the sinking kind of inevitable as if the two ships in the whole of the Atlantic had been drawn together at this singular location as if by a magnet of fate. Despite hours and hours of testimony after the accident, despite years now of analysis by maritime experts, no one was sure to ever be completely precise on just how it happened. Not even those in the bridge of either liner at the time.

Diving the Doria, Jenna could not help thinking of the ship's former beauty and magnificence even as she looked at the desolation of it all now. In the back of her mind, all her years of studying the shipwreck came to the fore. She thought of the last planning meeting with the others on board Explorer II and what she had said to them. "We do know that on the evening of July 25, 1956, two passenger ships were converging on a point southwest of the Nantucket Lightship, which marks the entry to and exit from the crowded approach to New York harbor. The 697-foot-long Andrea Doria, carrying a nearly full complement of 1,706 passengers and crew, was nearing the end of a mostly sunny and uneventful nine-day voyage from Genoa to New York. The Stockholm, at 528 feet in length and only 12,165 tons, one of the smallest of the new postwar liners, was just beginning its homeward voyage to Sweden. On the Andrea Doria's bridge, overseeing the work of the two senior officers on the watch, stood 58-year-old Captain Piero Calamai, a veteran of 39 years at sea and hundreds of Atlantic crossings. On the bridge of the Stockholm, the ship's youthful third officer, 26-year-old Johan-Ernst Bogislaus Carstens-Johannsen, was in charge of the 8:30 to 12:00 p.m. watch. It was standard policy in the Swedish Line, as on most liners, for only one officer and two seamen to stand each bridge watch."

Sam at the same moment below in the kitchen area now was having similar thoughts about the way Doria met her fate. At 10:20 p.m., the Andrea Doria came abeam of the Nantucket Lightship, and Captain Calamai ordered a new course that aimed directly at the Ambrose Lightship, which marks the mouth of New York harbor. The two ships were now approaching on roughly parallel courses, but being still beyond the range of each other's radar were as yet unaware of each other's presence. To complicate matters, the Andrea Doria was steaming in fog, while the Stockholm sailed through a clear night bathed in moonlight. Carstens-Johannsen had no inkling of the fogbank that lay just ahead.

In the corridor nearing the ballroom that Jake Stoughton wanted to explore anew, he too was having similar thoughts on the demise of the ship, here, now while in the belly of the beast. Given the circumstances on the night of Doria's demise neither ship was exercising maximum caution. Since mid-afternoon, the Andrea Doria had been steaming through patchy fog, at times dense enough to make the bow invisible from the bridge, but Captain Calamai had reduced speed only a little. He had a schedule to keep, and he was confident that his radar would alert him in ample time to avoid any problems.

He had, however, ordered various standard fog precautions: A lookout was posted in the bow and the watertight doors were closed. On the approach, the Stockholm had as yet no reason to reduce speed, but they had every reason to expect fog in the waters south of Nantucket Island, where the frigid Labrador Current met the warm Gulf Stream. The ship traveled to the north of the recommended sea lanes on a course likely to bring them into contact with incoming ships. After all, it was one of the busiest sea lanes in the world. No doubt Stockholm, like all of the liners didn't wish to take the recommended route twenty miles south of the Nantucket Lightship, because it added distance and time. Besides, Captain Gunnar Nordenson saw no reason to join his third officer on the bridge. Third Officer Carstens-Johannsen, known to his crewmates as Carstens, was perfectly capable of navigating the ship, even in these treacherous waters, as long as the weather stayed clear.

Jake shook off the thoughts of how the Doria lost its way. He told himself this was no time for such grim thoughts, not here, not now. There was plenty of time for that topside or on the long ascent while clinging to the guideline. He needed to concentrate on the task at hand. What he'd come for—the remains of a good man and fellow diver. Jenna might be in it for all the wrong reasons, and he guiltily shared some of those reasons, but more important to him now was the family who'd hired them—to give them closure, a body to bury, even if not entirely fleshed out any longer. To this end, he went back to work. He'd marked his path into the ballroom with strobe lights as he went. This deep in, one could take no chances.

He looked around at the spacious interior of the ballroom. He could imagine the music playing till the end, and dancers on the floor that night. He pictured the late-nighters, those who refused to waste their last night on the cruise merely sleeping. They wanted to be on hand for the midnight buffet, the music, conversation, and dancing. For a moment, Jake thought he could hear the music, the band, the dance noise from the semi-crowded floor at the hour of impact, then the suddenly loud clatter of instruments, chairs, and tables being thrown across the ship like so many children's toys. All phantom sounds just careening around in his head. He was reminded of times he'd visited Civil War battlefields like Shiloh, standing there and hearing the roar of cannons and the terrible cries of dying men drowned out by horses tearing about with wagons and cannon to move forward. As he stared into the ballroom, the same sort of sounds came to mind. The noise of course at a subdued level, just his imagination at work, when he heard his name called in a whisper that was louder than any of the back-scatter. Jacob…Jacob…come in.

It startled him, the sheer reality of it. It had come as clear as a ringing bell. He looked the entire room over, his arms and legs moving, fearful it was somehow Jenna and she was in trouble. Not here in the empty ballroom but in one of the compartments the other side of the ship. Certainly, Sharky had been right about the ballroom. No floating bodies here but the ghosts he'd conjured up swirling about in his head. But if Jenna was in trouble and sending out a psychic call for help, that couldn't have been any clearer. As a result, Jake swam away from his strobe lights and path out to the other side of the ballroom to find the near buried promenade deck there, going for the shattered staterooms near the stern, going for Jenna.

Jenna was absorbed in the crustacean life harbored here inside the ship, fascinated by the movement of the creatures and glad that she was larger than anything else in the shattered stateroom she had managed to get to. It would not be difficult, she told herself, for any diver, no matter his or her experience to become caught on something here and trapped as time and air ran out. It was possible that Pritchards, for whatever reason, was enticed down the very path she was enticed to follow this moment.

Behind her somewhere, she heard her name being called. It was Jake and he sounded in a panic, a panic for her. He was breaking up, and from topside, she could make out Jim Hollande telling him he was sucking in too much oxygen and to calm down. What's happened, she wondered, turned to see Jake rushing far too carelessly toward her. She glanced back at the beckoning compartment ahead, the last of the shattered area where the nose of the Stockholm had obliterated so much of the superstructure here. She truly believed that Pritchards would be found just around the next pile of debris.

"Are you all right, Jenna? I heard you call my name."

"I'm perfectly fine, and I did not call your name."

Hollande from overhead confirmed that Jenna had made no outcry for help. Jake shrugged. "Found nothing in the ballroom, but I could've sworn—"

"I'm determined to make it from here to the next stateroom," she cut him off. "I have a strong hunch."

"Take the corridor to your left. Much safer."

"No time." She rushed on, squeezing in and around shaky debris.

"You are taking far too many chances, Jenna, and time's running low."

She ignored him and moved on. He followed with more caution, his size bumping things more than she had. "This is good your being with me when I discover Pritchards."

"You're that sure?"

"Something keeps telling me he's here somewhere."

"Same as Sam with the kitchen area, and me with the ballroom, I guess."

"They were in the last destroyed compartment, the gaping hole now a wall of silt and sand as the port side of the ship was jammed into the ocean bottom. But there was no body here, no bones, nothing of Pritchards.

"Sorry, Jenna. What'ayasay we get back to the guideline."

She sighed and nodded, disappointed. "Best we follow my strobe light path out, Jake."

"No, no—across the ballroom and back to my lights. Much faster. Look at your Trimix level."

She did so and decided he was right. The two of them hurried from the site of the crash back the way Jake had come, crossing the ballroom, hurrying until suddenly Jenna stopped moving and stared at something Jake could not see. "What is it?"

"Odd…thought I saw dancers, and not happy dancers."

76

"Imagining things?"

"Jake, places of high trauma, sudden death, souls get trapped, but this one dancer, actually a few, they're wearing dive suits."

Jake stared to where she looked. Nothing. "Let's get out of here, kiddo, now. Time is up."

He took her by the wrist and pulled her along. They quickly found the strobe lights he'd attached to monitor his dive to this location. "I hope Sam's doing better than us," he complained as they rushed along the promenade now.

"Oh my god, Jake, look at that thing going by." They could see out into the sea now, and what was lolling about the shipwreck was a monster squid, a giant. These creatures had been known to eat killer whales. They wouldn't hesitate to swallow a man or a woman whole.

They quickly realized they were hostages here for the moment. It would be suicide to race back to the tether line and hang there for over an hour while slowly ascending with a giant squid curious about them. "We need to warn Sam," Jake said even as she was doing just that, telling Jim to relay the news as his relay from the dive boat might be clearer than hers.

"Sam had the same amount of air supply as the others, and he was well aware that his time in the kitchen area was up. He'd searched three of the four freezers to no avail, but he hadn't time left to search further. It was damnably frustrating, and now he had the news about some damn giant squid guarding the ship. He was directed to join Jenna and Jake at their location and pray that the beast outside would become bored and move on.

"Need a school of sharks to come along and chase that mother off," Sam said as he made his way back to the surface, following his strobe light path, leaving them in place for another attempt tomorrow. As he did so, he heard his name called in a tender, endearing manner. It almost sounded like a little child, a girl's voice. Not Jenna's whiskey voice at all. It kept repeating his name now like a mantra: Sam…Sam…Sam…stay with me.

"Honey, nothin' personal but I'm getting the hell out of here," he replied.

Jim upstairs asked him what he was talking about? "Your vitals looking good, but who're you talking to?"

Jenna was asking questions too. "Sam, you OK?"

Jake added, "Get to us, Sam, now. Maybe the three of us, using our ugly looks, can scare that monster off."

"Time's just about up, guys! monster squid or not, you have to get on the line and begin your ascent."

"Damn, some choice. Devoured by a sea monster or end it like Pritchards and so many others on the Doria." Jake wanted to pound a fist into something, but in this watery environment, it would only be an ineffective tap.

"Jim," asked Jenna. "Is it still nestling in around the ship? We can't see it."

78

"Jenna, the cameras are on your head. If you can't see it, then I can't see it."

"But you got some great shots of that thing, right?"

"For sure, yes."

"Good."

"Jenna it's no time to be worried about your documentary," said Jake. "It's time to worry about your life."

"The play's the thing, eh, Jenna?" asked Sam, chuckling.

"We have no choice, guys," Jake said, staring at his gauge. "I saw we all three go at once and pray the damn thing is either asleep or looking the other way."

Jake started out, fully expecting the other two to follow. He glanced back. Sam and Jenna were gabbing, hesitating. Jake, angry now, gestured for them to come ahead. He could not see the squid anywhere. It had moved over the ship and had kept going so far as he could tell. He gave his two partners the all-clear sign. Then he rushed to his strobe light on the line, thinking the other two had better be right behind him now. When he got to the line and turned around, holding on and beginning his ascent, he saw that Sam and Jenna were now on his heels. This allowed him to sigh and continue his escape from certain death.

The three divers now began climbing, and all settled in for the long, arduous trek to the surface. It was not simply 250 odd feet, but the necessary stops to decompress that took so much time. In some

79

cases an hour and fifteen minutes. During this time, Jake began thinking of what he'd experienced in the ballroom, and then how Jenna had stopped cold in that room, staring off into space, claiming she could see the dead and they were dancing in that place as if a metaphor for death. After a time, as he climbed to the next ten feet, Jake began thinking of the ship itself and its grim history. He recalled reading about how the Andrea Doria's radar had a slightly greater range than the Stockholm's, and how the Doria bridge crew detected an oncoming ship at about 10:45 p.m. the foggy night of her doom. The other ship was at a distance of about 17 nautical miles.

Curzio Franchini, the ship's second officer, alerted the captain, and Calamai immediately requested the other ship's bearing. She was only four degrees off the starboard bow—in other words, almost dead ahead. This information didn't worry the Andrea Doria's captain or the two watch officers on the bridge. There was ample time and distance to pass the oncoming vessel with plenty of room. They had done so a thousand times before with a thousand other ships. Only one important decision needed to be made—whether to pass the ship to port or starboard. According to Franchini, the oncoming ship continued to bear slight to the right, causing Captain Calamai to suspect the blip had to be a small coastal vessel that would soon turn north to Nantucket.

At the same time, on board the Stockholm, Third Officer Carstens saw things quite differently. He had just picked up a blip on his radar indicating a ship 12 nautical miles away and slightly to his port. Acting according to standard Swedish line procedure, he plotted the course of the oncoming vessel, which required two radar fixes. By the time he'd completed his calculations, the other ship was fewer than six miles away. It appeared set to pass to the north, but by less than a mile. As soon as the other ship came into view, Carstens thought, I'll alter course to starboard, so as to increase the width of our passing distance.

After several minutes, he began to wonder why the other ship's lights failed to appear. He could still see the moon and the possibility he was sailing into a fogbank seems to have not occurred to him. Those navigating the two ships were now racing toward one another at a combined speed of roughly 40 knots, and both had somehow come to opposite conclusions. Aboard the Andrea Doria, the approaching ship seemed to be maintaining a position just off the starboard bow. According to the Stockholm's radar, the other vessel seemed clearly to be a few degrees to port and on a parallel course. One of the radar sets, or one of the men who read them, was wrong.

Jake had always condemned the men in charge, all of them, but given the state of radar at the time, and the fact that no ship kept a perfect, steady course, small errors quickly became large, larger, then huge. On board the Andrea Doria, such an error might have been caught, had someone bothered to plot the oncoming ship's course instead of relying on an eyeball estimate from the radar screen, but on the Italian Line such calculations were not routine practice. The men in command on both ships seemed to have had more faith in their radar, and their ability to interpret it, than they should have.

This faith led Captain Calamai to make òne of his most controversial decisions of the night. He decided to pass the approaching vessel starboard side to starboard side. Standard procedure, when two ships meet at sea, is for a port side to port side passing. But the Andrea Doria's skipper assumed there was good reason this night for making an exception. The other ship was already to starboard, or so he believed. A port-side passing would mean crossing her bow and sailing closer to more heavily traveled coastal waters. Given the wide and empty ocean to his left, it seemed natural to stray from standard procedure. About 11:05 p.m., with the other ship about three and a half nautical miles away, Captain Calamai ordered a small four-degree course change to port to increase the passing distance. Neither ship had yet seen the other, except on radar.

Jenna was just below Jake on the tether line, and she too had gone from wondering what she had psychically witnessed in the ballroom on this dive, and what she had felt the day before on their first dive. But after exhausting her wonderment and her astonishment at what could only be called a haunted shipwreck, she began what felt like shared thoughts from another source; thoughts on the night the Andrea Doria was stove in by the Stockholm.

Just as the Andrea Doria changed course, the two ships finally made visual contact. With only two miles now separating them, a perilously short distance, given their combined speed, they were converging at a slight angle, so that the Andrea Doria saw lights to its right, while the Stockholm finally saw lights to its left. Thus the first sight of the other ship only reinforced the false assumptions on each bridge: that the other vessel was where it was expected. On the Stockholm's bridge, Carstens now issued an order he might more wisely have given long before—a sharp turn to starboard to give the oncoming ship a wider berth. Unfortunately for him, Captain Calamai remained convinced the Stockholm would pass him safely starboard to starboard. Without realizing it, Carstens was turning his ship toward the Andrea Doria's course. And he failed to signal his turn with the usual blasts on the ship's whistle. Then the bridge telephone rang, and he turned away to answer it.

For a split second, Captain Calamai couldn't believe what he was seeing. With the approaching ship only a mile away, its masthead lights had clearly materialized from the fog for him to visually determine its true course. He watched intently as the lower navigation light crossed from right to left in front of the higher one. To his horror, the other ship was turning right! Then the red light appeared, indicating the ship was showing its port side, confirming the worst. Third Officer Eugenio Giannini had seen it too. "She is turning, she is turning!" he'd shouted. "She is coming toward us."

All thirty-nine of Captain Calamai's years at sea surely passed in front of his eyes in the instant before he called out his next order. "Tutto sinistra," he called out. "Full left." He immediately put all his faith in the Andrea Doria's speed and maneuverability, hoping to turn left faster than the other ship was turning right. But a huge ocean liner going full speed did not turn like a Ferrari.

On board the Stockholm, Carstens brought his gaze back from the bridge telephone call from the crow's nest telling him what he already knew. At this point, he still assumed all ahead of his ship was fine. The lights of a ship were visible 20 degrees to port, but Carstens had turned away to take that call just as the other ship had begun its hard left turn. It took him a few moments to grasp what was happening when the realization hit him hard: Whoever the hell that is, the other liner has turned across our bow! He wrenched the handle of the engine telegraph to full astern and shouted to his helmsman, "Hard-a-starboard!" It was too little, too late.

Had Captain Calamai turned right instead of left, he might well have avoided a collision or minimized its impact. A glancing blow head to head is less damaging than a broadside ramming, but that is what the Andrea Doria received. The bow of the Stockholm plunged into the Italian liner's starboard hull plates just aft of her bridge, ripping open seven of her 11 decks, the hole reaching almost down to her keel. For a moment, the smaller ship lodged there like a stopper in a bottle, then the force of the

84

water rushing past the Andrea Doria's hull, as she was still moving at almost full speed, tore the Stockholm away. A torrent of seawater began to pour through the gaping hole in the Italian liner's hull. The time was just past 11:10 p.m.

CHAPTER SEVEN

What is this death but a negligible accident?

Sam Kent had been telling himself he'd had an oxygen deprivation hallucination below him at the Andrea Doria, an auditory hallucination. He'd not seen her. He'd only heard her. The voice of a young girl, high-pitched, asking nicely for him to stay. He could imagine Pritchards, on hearing a young person's voice inside the shipwreck going toward that voice, losing track of his time, paying no attention to his gauges. Sam worked to put it out of mind for now. Nothing to do about it. His last thought on the eerie experience was that he could easily have overstayed his welcome, and very nearly had done just that. On account of the hallucination. For now, Jake at the lead was a mere twenty feet from the surface, Jenna thirty, and he was breathing easy at a mere forty feet from the surface. They could also see daylight overhead. It was now that Jake's thoughts turned to the night Doria suffered her doom.

Sam had always thought it was poignantly sad that the ship was so close to its destination, as the Andrea Doria had been scheduled to dock in New York early the following morning, and because of its being her last night out, many of the ship's 1,134 passengers, especially those with young children, had already retired. But the moment of collision caught quite a few passengers engaged in last night entertainments. The dance band in the first-class Belvedere Room nightclub had launched into yet another rendition of Arrivederci, Roma, when it literally tumbled off its podium amid a clatter of instruments as dancing couples toppled to the floor. In the tourist-class dining room, where passengers were enjoying a Jane Russell movie called Foxfire, the screen went dead and a short-lived panic erupted in the darkness. Throughout the ship, those who hadn't yet gone to bed rushed to their staterooms, awoke sleeping children, grabbed life jackets and a few belongings, then headed for their muster stations. For within minutes of the impact, the Andrea Doria had taken on an alarming list to starboard.

Those passengers already in their cabins when the collision happened fared very differently, depending on where their quarters were located. On the port side, the worst experience was to be thrown out of bed or off one's feet. Fourteen-year-old Madge Young, who was brushing her teeth in the bathroom of her first-class stateroom on the portside upper deck, heard the terrible crash like an explosion as she fell into the bathtub with no harm done. But in cabin 56 on the starboard side, in which the Young family had originally been booked, Thure Peterson actually glimpsed the Stockholm's hull slide past him before he lost consciousness. When he came to, he discovered his wife, Martha trapped beneath ugly wreckage, and despite heroic efforts to free her by Peterson and a steward named Giovanni Rovelli and the ministrations of Dr. Bruno Tortari Donati, Mrs. Peterson eventually died from her bloody injuries.

In retrospect, some escapees seemed blessed or at least extremely lucky. Some escapes felt absolutely miraculous, but none more so than that of fourteen-year-old young woman named Linda Morgan, whose mother was trapped in cabin 54. Asleep in cabin 52, only two doors down from the unfortunate Petersons, Linda Morgan had somehow been catapulted out of her bed and onto the Stockholm's crushed bow, where a crewman heard her calling for her mother, with whom she was eventually reunited. However, Linda's sleeping little Lorena Morgan, upset at having to go to bed so early as she'd pleaded to stay in the first class ballroom to hear more music and to dance the final night on board away, Lorena, weeping in her bed over her mother's unfairness toward her while she'd allowed Linda another hour at the dance, Lorena was instantly killed.

The girls' father was in New York, awaiting his family's return home when he got the news. A news reporter, he'd been reporting on the news and had learned of the family's fate, and Linda was dubbed by the media as the miracle girl, while sister Lorena went largely ignored by the press and the world as her story was no miracle. Some 49 others on board had also lost their lives.

When Sam followed Jenna up and onto Explorer II, he was still wondering about that twelve-year-old girl, Lorena Morgan, and so was

Jenna, and so was Jake. They were unaware of it just yet, but they were having a number of shared thoughts. Quite detailed shared thoughts.

Dolph Nielsen first and then Jim Hollande welcomed the divers back on board. "The approach of the storm," Jim informed them "has mercifully turned in our favor, so that the boat is hardly rocking and the white caps have scurried off."

Dolph and Jim helped each diver with the equipment and dressing down as each arrived on deck at ten and fifteen minute intervals. As with any deep water dive, Jim was relieved to see all three back in good health and no one coughing his guts out. Some light-headedness, a bit of deep breathing of sea air, a bit of getting feeling back in their nerves, but all-in-all, it had been a successful dive except for the elephant on board: They had not located the prize they'd gone after—Thom Pritchards' remains. With the old adage of time is money, everyone knew they had only one more day, and even now other dive boats had come into their space to make their own excursions to the shipwreck, complicating matters.

Still, the only one on board Explorer II who could dive tonight was Jim, and he'd be alone save for the excursion divers already on and inside the Doria. Without a safety partner, the risks of his going in search of Pritchards was too high everyone thought, except Jim. He insisted he could make the dive and search out that last freezer compartment that Sam hadn't had time to get to. Jenna argued that Jim had editing work to do tonight on the footage they had, and that she desperately wanted to go over every frame with him. "It's not the kind of work, Jake or Sam care about, not like you, Jim. Come on, stay with me."

But Jim was adamant about going down, and when she saw him glance at Sharky and Jake, she realized that it was a man thing. But suddenly, Jake said to Jim, "Don't go. Not alone, Jim. There's more to worry about down there than…than you might realize."

"What's that supposed to mean?"

"Tell him, Jenna. I know you saw something," Jake said.

"Hold on, all of you," began Sam. "Let's all get a cup of coffee and a bite to eat, and let's share what happened on that dive."

"What are you all talking about?" asked Jim.

"Just don't suit up right now, Jim," said Jenna. "Hear us out."

After they were all seated around the mess table, having coffee and a hearty meal, Jake said, "Jim, are you telling me you saw nothing unusual on our cameras down there?"

"No, nothing out of the ordinary, no."

"These things don't normally show up on cameras," Jenna said.

"What sort of things are you two talking about?" asked Jim.

"Spirits," replied Jenna.

"What? Spirits?" Jim looked about to see who was in on the joke.

90

"Spirits, ghosts, revenants, whatever you want to call them, but that ship is haunted," Jenna said.

Sam finally added, "I heard a voice, and it was not inside my head. The voice of a child, a young girl, inviting me to stay. Happened in the kitchen area where I was searching, but only after I was damn near out of air. In my mind's eye, I got the concept of a white blond-haired pale as death snow white, a little princess of the castle. Crazy, huh? Felt her even more as I was ascending like she was someone I remembered from somewhere."

"There's definitely something down there," added Jake. "I felt it, and Jenna, she saw what I felt. Didn't you, Jenna?"

"I saw dead people dancing in the ballroom, yes, and while some were in the garb of 1956, others, Jim...they were in dive suits."

Jim reacted in knee-jerk fashion, still thinking the three of them had cooked all this up for him. "So, did you see Pritchards at the dance?"

"Hard to tell, the divers were wearing full gear."

"They died with their tanks on, eh?" Jim continued to make light of what the others were saying.

"Look, Jim," began Jake, "we're all trying to make sense of the feelings, the sounds, the sights we witnessed down there. This is not a put up job. Something's alive—in some manner of nature or super-nature on the Andrea Doria. Some force of nature we may not understand but there it is."

91

"You're serious about this? All three of you?"

"I felt it on yesterday's dive," Jenna confessed. "But it was just a feeling of like, well, being watched, and she's called out to me as well. Only a few words but they were audible."

Jake then confessed, "Me too, asking me to come in to the ballroom."

Sam then said, "I think she's Linda Morgan's sister, Lorena...the one who died instantly on impact."

"That's curious," said Jake. "I had the same thought."

"Me as well," added Jenna. "As if the idea was planted in my brain."

But the concept of a ghostly pale, blond-haired, blue-eyed little doll of a girl enticing divers to their deaths in the Andrea Doria remained too much for Jim Hollande to accept. "All very interesting guys," he began, "but I want to know what's in door number four in the galley on board, and I'm not going to any dance."

"After all we've said, and you're going to dive alone tonight, Jim?" asked Jake. "Look man, tomorrow, Sam mans the cameras, and you, me, and Jenna together."

Jim looked at Sam. "You OK with that, Sharky?"

"I am. Not sure I am as curious of that last walk-in as I am fearful of some hoo-doo voodoo that little siren can put on a man, hypnosis is the closest thing I can describe it as."

92

"Well I am damn curious what's in the fourth freezer compartment."

"Most likely more hanging beef and pork, my friend."

"And what if Pritchards' body is in there like you theorized originally?"

Sam smiled at Jim. "Then all the glory goes to you, Jim. I think seventeen deaths attributed to the Doria is warning enough for this old man, especially after hearing that specter down there."

"I agree with Sam, Jim," said Jake. "She's a siren of sorts, this girl. She may not be evil; hell, she may be innocent as the day she was born and the day she died, but she is dangerous."

"She gets in your head, Jim," added Jenna.

Jim realized now that his friends and colleagues were not pulling his leg but deadly serious. And he'd heard enough. "All right, no night dive for me. Tomorrow with dive partners it is."

"Smart move, Jim," Sam assured him. "Just don't want you to become number eighteen. For a moment down there, I thought the number was going to go to twenty in one fell swoop."

Jake rose from his seat and slapped Jim on the shoulder. "Jimbo, good choice. I'm now convinced that a lot of the behavior exhibited by those who'd died rushing the ascent, or of a heart attack while on the tether, or just within reach of the boat occurred as much from fright as from being ill-trained or in ill-health."

"On that note, I'm going to bed," said Jenna.

"We could all use some rest," agreed Sam.

93

"Sleep…perchance to dream?" asked Jim with a little shake of his head. "You guys dream awake."

"Trust us, Jim. There is something alive—in some eerie sense—on the Andrea Doria, and it has taken seventeen lives to date."

"I got it…I got it."

Jim Hollande couldn't sleep. He'd rolled over countless times. He didn't want to sleep. He wanted to know if there was anything worth a look in Sam's final fourth walk-in freezer. It took tons of food and meats to feed the 1,770 hundred passengers and crew aboard the Doria, proven by all the ugly forests of hanging meat in the three freezers they had footage on from Sam's trek to the galley. But Sam had great instincts on land and in the water. Jim couldn't shake the idea that they would find Pritchards' frozen body inside door number four.

Perhaps Thom Pritchards, curious himself about what might be salvaged from a freezer compartment inside the Doria, an overlooked one, had placed a piece of debris as a door jam, but the item hadn't done the job. Suppose he was trapped inside? Just waiting for someone to discover his perfectly preserved body? Jim imagined the headlines, what such a find would do for their film project, not to mention closure for the family. An intact body to bury.

He looked at the clock on his night stand. It read: 2:38AM. Everyone else was asleep. All his gear was ready and waiting. He could do the dive, film his progress, check out the freezer for good or naught, and be back before the others even knew he'd been away. He could take the flak from them later, and if he was successful? Glory be, he told himself.

"To hell with ghosts, too," he said to the empty state room, pushed up and off the bed. Still in his skivvies, he went for his dive suit and equipment. No one saw him drop over the side, but Jenna heard the splash as she'd also been unable to sleep and was star-gazing on the other side of the Explorer.

She rushed to the sound of the splash. Curious as to its source, Jenna searched the water off the portside, but all she could see were bubbles. Bubbles coming from a diver. She looked across at two excursion boats bobbing on the waves, wondering if it could be one of their divers who'd somehow followed the wrong tether line and was about to surface and board the Explorer. She waited to welcome the diver, but after a time, she realized that whoever it was, he or she was not surfacing. Whoever it was he wasn't coming but going. He'd dropped from the Explorer.

She then went a few steps to her left to inspect the diving gear. There were only three sets staring back at her: Jake's, Sam's and her own. "Damn you, Jim Hollande!" she shouted and rushed to wake the others. Along the corridor of state rooms below, she stopped to slam open Jim's door. The sight of his empty bunk cinched it. "He's gone and done it!" she shouted down the hallway, pushing open Sam's door, then Jake's. The two men leapt up from their slumber and the three huddled in the slightly more spacious corridor.

"Are you sure?"

"Yes, he's gone to the wreck."

"We've gotta suit up, catch up to him," Jake insisted.

"You need more hours out of the water, Jake," Sam cautioned. "And he knows that."

"Why would he do this, Sam?" asked Jenna. "Why? After all our warnings, all three of us?"

"Apparently, he's playing the hero in your docudrama," said Dolph Nielsen, the chief engineer, who'd been awakened by all the commotion. "Look, I have deep diving experience. He shrugged, "No equipment, however I'm about your size, Jake. How about I go partner with the damn fool? Nobody should ever do a deep water dive alone."

The others considered Dolph's offer, and Sam asked, "I take it then you're checked out at those depths?"

"Many times over, Sam, yes."

"Great. No way any of us can go down until at least six or seven AM."

Dolph said, "It's just turning three now." The Norwegian, stood tall, muscular, young and eager to help. The others were eager to have his help. "He's got five, ten minutes on you, Dolph," said Jenna.

"I can make up those minutes, descending."

"Not too fast," cautioned Sam. "You overdo it, and you'll be in a bad way and no help to Jim."

Jake looked Nielsen in the eyes. "Just see that he gets out of there before his air supply does. We'll be monitoring you both from the control room."

"And Dolph, be careful for yourself," said Sam. "There're forces down there that are natural dangers, yes, but there is also something else."

"Something else?" Dolph asked.

"What Sam's talking about, Dolph, is something all three of us experienced inside the wreck during our last dive. Something that wants divers to remain there."

"Dolph smiled and nodded. "Oh yes, I have had that feeling on more than one wreck dive. I know it well."

"Then just know that the force or whatever it is, is strong in the Andrea Doria," warned Jenna, a hand on Dolph's shoulder.

"Got it. Not to worry about Dolph. I am strong like bull," he joked.

"We'll be monitoring from the control room," Jake repeated himself as he rushed to find Jim Hollande on the monitors.

Fully geared up now, Dolph dropped over the side and began his descent to the Doria. Jenna watched until he was so deep that she could no longer see the bubbles rising. She turned to find that Sam had followed Jake. She rushed to join them in the control room. It was going to be a long and tense night.

In the depths below, Jim Hollande, who'd scrupulously studied Sam Kent's dive plan when

Sam first red-penciled it, had made no wrong turns in locating the galley, the rows of kitchens where the many chefs on board worked tirelessly to feed the hundreds of passengers and crew four times a day, breakfast, lunch, dinner, and the midnight buffet. The last of which had been so terribly disrupted. Jim had no trouble locating the four standing doors to the freezer compartments, the three left open to the current since Sam had been unable to push them closed against the pressure of the water by himself. Such work would have exhausted his air supply had he tried any harder than he had.

Then at the end of this row of opened, inspected freezer compartments stood the final one. Was Pritchards' body on the inside? Only one way to find out. Jim had turned his camera on during his descent, and he was giving a play-by-play for the film. He'd set the stage to record for Jenna and the project he believed in more passionately than anyone knew. He had also developed a passion for Jenna herself.

He'd been recording even as the others had stood about arguing over what to do when Dolph gave them a solution. Jim was now narrating where he was and building the drama of opening door #4. His thoughts told him that he'd edit this footage in behind Sam's three failed attempts at finding anything of Pritchards' remains in the first three doors. Jim knew instinctively that it'd make for great reality TV. Underwater reality TV.

From above came the chorus of warnings and pleas for him to take all precautions against any and all forces in the deep he might encounter. He was also told that a dive partner, Dolph Nielsen, was on his way to shadow his movements and monitor him first hand should anything untoward happen.

Jim thought it best to simply acknowledge that he'd gotten the message, adding, "I'm doing fine. Nothing to worry about. I am now going for door number four."

"Wait for backup, Jim. Wait for Dolph," Jenna pleaded.

"No need. I am sure he will be here soon, but given the limited time I have inside here, I have to act now and not waste a moment waiting for Dolph."

From above, they watched the camera image close in on the freezer compartment door. Sam quietly lamented, "Damn, I wanted to open that door so badly when I was down there but my time was up."

"Let's just hope Jim's time is not up," quipped Jake.

Jenna immediate scolded Jake for this.

"I didn't say I hope it would happen, Jenna. I said I hope it doesn't!"

"Given the eerie shit we ran into down there, it's not clever to say anything approximating—"

"Enough you two," chastised Sam. "It's hard enough following Jim without you two bickering over my shoulder."

"Sorry, Sam," Jenna said and Jake fell silent, and then he went back to monitoring Dolph's progress.

"How's Dolph doing?" Jenna asked Jake now.

"He's on the deck, going along the promenade for Sam's galley. He seems to really know the direction."

"Well he has dived her before," Sam said as Juan Carlos appeared with a pot of coffee and cups for them all.

"A life saver, Juan, thanks," said Jenna and the men thanked the cook as well.

"I couldn't sleep for all the noise. Trouble, eh?" he asked.

"That's an understatement," said Jake. "Got us a rouge diver down there thinks he's the Lone Ranger."

"Dolph?" the cook asked.

"No, Hollande," replied Sam. "We sent Dolph after him."

"Dolph wanted to dive is why I thought…"

"Dolph wanted to dive?" asked Jake, curious.

"Asked he if I dived and could use my gear."

"You don't dive, Juan."

"I think I know that, sir, but when I said no, he was looking kind of frustrated. I suggested he talk to you, Sam."

"Which he never did."

"Said someone had broken into his hotel room on the mainland and robbed him of his gear, and that he hadn't time to get anything new before it was time to shove off."

"Said all that did he?" asked Jake, curious.

"He seemed awfully anxious to go after Jim, didn't he?" asked Jake.

"Well, damn it, Jake, it's your show. You did the hiring. How much do you know about your chief engineer?"

"I couldn't get my usual man. He'd had an accident and was laid up. Nielsen showed up like a lucky penny just in time. I didn't have a whole lot of time to vet him, but he answered every one of my questions spot on. He knows his stuff."

The discussion ended when Jenna said, "Jim's about to open that door. Shut up, you two."

Hollander below, his camera angles too close and shaking now as he worked to pull the heavy freezer door open against the water, did so, and as it opened, the sealed compartment began filling with ocean water from the submerged galley. The rush, as when Sam had done the same with three other freezers, had a dramatic effect and the sound was an added nice touch for the video.

"Hope this isn't going to be like Geraldo's empty vault from the Titanic," said Sam.

"Or your three freezers, Sam," said Jake.

The three more experienced divers fell silent as Hollande now started into the freezer compartment. It dawned on them all and likely Jim knew that had Pritchards had entered this place, it would have taken an underwater tsunami to close that door behind him. Either that or a supernatural force.

"With Dolph coming up the rear," said Jenna, "should that door close, at least Dolph's there to open it."

"I went in and out of three of those walk-ins," said Sam, "and nothing closed any door behind me."

"Maybe the ghosts aren't interested in an old sea dog like you, Sam," said Jake.

"Too salty, eh?" Sam replied and laughed. "But on my way out, I tell you, I clearly heard that child's voice, enticing me to stay."

"At the time you were exploring those compartments, Sam, she may well have been engaged...curious about Jake and me." Jenna sipped at her hot coffee, replenished by Juan.

The three of them were now fixed on Jim's camera as he explored the freezer. It looked no different than the previous three that Sam had explored. Animal carcasses dangling from meat hooks, lambs, pigs, cows, pheasants, all manner of floating boxes of supplies now.

"No sign of Pritchards is there, Jim?" Sam asked.

"Going to the far wall, Sam. Not giving up yet. If his body was in her, with that influx of rushing water, it would have slammed him to the rear."

"Watching your time?" Sam asked him.

"On it, Sam. Not a problem."

As Jim progressed toward the rear, Jenna asked, "Where the hell's Dolph?"

"He's entering the galley area now," replied Jim. "Vitals look good but rising."

"Hey Jimbo," said Jake, calling down to him. "Dolph's going to take over for you. Your Trimix is getting dangerously low, and you still have to climb out of there."

"I just want to finish what I started, Jake."

"Sure, sure but when Dolph reaches you, tag-team it, man."

Jim hesitated replying but finally said, "Sure…sure, Jakie." Then came a sudden spike in Jim's vital signs.

Sam seeing this and studying the live feed, suddenly shouted, "What in hell is that, Jim?"

Jim had stopped cold, his camera recording a row of human carcasses on meat hooks. Jim had frozen in place, staring at the sight. From above the human shapes inside the plastic wrappings could be made out. They looked like mannequins.

"How many are there, Jim?" asked Sam.

"Four, four," Jim croaked.

Dolph came up alongside Jim and snatched at his camera, and both camera's went down. There was a struggle picked up on audio. "You're Trimix, Jim! It's low. You've got to get back, now! Now!"

"You have no right! Get away!" came Jim's voice.

"Do what Dolph says, Jim! Get out," Sam shouted down to him.

Jenna added, "Dolph's got more air than you, Jim. Turn it over to him, now! That's an order!"

The vital signs of both men had spiked wildly. Then Jim's camera returned, and he was in the galley, outside the freezer, frantically rushing back to the tether line. He'd become so involved in his search for Pritchards, and then finding the secret stash of bodies inside here that he'd become careless."

"Dolph, you have only five or six minutes inside there," began Jake, "and then you've got to move as well. Turn your g'damn camera back on, man!"

"Jesus, you don't think Jim's hurt Dolph, do you?" asked Jenna as all of them wondered why Dolph had gone silent, his camera still down.

"Dolph, come in, Dolph, now!"

"Get your video up and going!"

"What's going on, Dolph, Dolph?"

Suddenly, the video went from snow to the face of someone long dead, a male, or what appeared his death mask. It was an aged man with hoarfrost coloring his features. Then the camera panned to a second dead man on a hook. Both men were wrapped in thick plastic coverings, but their faces had been exposed by someone using a dive knife. Someone who'd come ahead of Nielsen. Then he came to a third body, also painted by hoarfrost but definitely a younger man than the other two.

Then Dolph panned to the eerie image of a frozen woman, and after tearing away the plastic wrap further from her face, Dolph stared into the features. Who was she? No Mussolini, no mummies. Just four ordinary enough looking people, all stony cold and hard as statues. Were they executed here or was this something even more

104

sinister than a mafiosi fulfilling a series of contract killings?

Using his dive knife, Dolph ripped a jagged tear straight down the frozen plastic, directly down the front of the female, and as he did so, he discovered a frost-covered identity plate dangling about the deceased's neck that read: Inge Viermetz. Born 7 March 1908. Aschaffenburg, Germany.

Dolph gasped, sucking in his air supply. He knew the name from his studies of the Nazi hunters. This woman's death was unknown, but she was responsible for the Lebsenborn situated in Nazi Germany as assistant to Max Sollmann, head of the Lebensborn—the Nazi run orphanage for abducted Polish children whose features fit the Aryan mold. She had been acquitted after the war, released, and had disappeared from history.

Now she's here, Dolph thought, staring into the at the stone, cold image of the dead woman. But who then were the three men? What were they all doing in a meat freezer dangling from hooks on a ship bound for America?

Dolph glances at his dive watch, checking his time. He didn't have enough, but he had to know the identities of the dead. With his dive knife, he tore away at the other plastic wrapped corpses to at least have their names to determine more about them later. The first he learned was Siegfried Handloser, a German physician, date of death 1954. Another was Hugo Eckener, German inventor and commander of the famous Graf Zeppelin during its record-setting flights. But the man had died at 88 years of age and there had been an open casket, a parade of thousands at his funeral, so how did his body come to be here? Finally, the last identifying plate around the last neck read: Enrico Fermi.

"It can't be," Dolph said into his com-link, realizing that those above were also seeing what he was seeing. "Fermi…the most famous Italian in history? The nuclear physicist, Father of the Atom Bomb."

"Didn't he die on American soil of stomach cancer?" said Jake from above.

"That's always been the story, but apparently not," replied Dolph. "Gone at age fifty-three as I recall."

Dolph Nielsen was suddenly inundated with questions from everyone monitoring events from above, but he shouted back, "I don't have time for a question and answer session right here and now. I'm running low on air. Am turning back." But suddenly Dolph was jostled as his camera attested, and he shouted an obscenity in his native language that Jake had heard him use while working on a jammed hoisting winch on their way out to the dive site.

"What's going on, Dolph?"

"It's him, Pritchards! First to discover Fermi and this gang of dead beats here. It must have cost Thom his life." Dolph's camera now clearly showed a man in complete diving gear, floating and bobbing, face down, then up, onto his side, then rolling with the slight current that'd been created when the freezer was opened to the inrush of water.

106

Pritchards' mask remained on, disguising his features, but he'd been perfectly preserved inside the freezer. How the water had gone out of the freezer from Pritchards' original visit was a mystery- within-a-mystery. The water possibly drained out through a system placed on board for the defrosting of the place.

How the four carcasses had gotten here in 1956 proved a more provocative mystery than the plumbing and the pipes within the coils of the Andrea Doria.

"Get back, Dolph," Jenna said. "Get outta there, now!"

"Your vitals are spiking." Sam beat a fist on the console.

Jake shouted over the others, "Dolph, get to the tether line, now!"

"Not to worry. As you American's say, I'm out of here."

"Where's Jim?" asked Jenna of Sam.

"Damn fool is still in the galley. He's lingering there, staring back at the freezer door, and the damn door is closing on Dolph.

Jim was shouting for Dolph to get out as the door was slowly about to seal him in the tomb. From Jim's camera, those above saw Dolph just squeeze through what was left of a sliver of escape as the door slammed shut, water pressure or no water pressure.

Jim, seeing Dolph free of the tomb, turned and began making his way out of the labyrinth that was

Sam's original route into and out of the galley with Dolph on his heels.

CHAPTER EIGHT

*Why should I be out of mind because I
am out of sight?*

Jim took the lead on the tether line as his trimix was terribly depleted. No one knew why he'd stopped and stared back at that closing door, and he was not saying but rather concentrating hard on survival now. He had to slow his breathing and fight against panic. As he ascended, he could switch over to pure oxygen and take deep breaths, but if he ascended too quickly for this prize, the bends could kill him. His heart was racing as it was from what he'd seen in the galley. He must slow his mind and control his heart if he wished to live, but this was no small feat.

From upstairs, Sam kept going on about how bad his vital signs were looking. In other words, how bad his chances looked. He finally calmly, firmly asked Sam to "Keep it to yourself, old man! Don't tell me the odds!"

Sam understood, shut up, and worried in silence over what the monitor was telling them all. Meanwhile, Dolph had ascended more quickly and had caught up to Jim on the tether line and pulled his mouthpiece from him and shoved his own into Jim's mouth. This allowed Jim a little more time on the Trimix. Ten feet more and you can go on oxygen, Jim. It's in your reach. Hold on," Dolph said to him.

Jim's eyes had been rolling back in his head, and his grip on the tether had loosened. Had not Dolph shared what he had, Jim would have let go and floated off to his death to become the eighteenth good man to not return from the Andrea Doria.

Jim made it to the next ten feet and the pure oxygen. Breathing it in felt like a rebirth for him. His vital signs above leveled off. Jenna had some stunning video of the Norwegian Nielsen saving the American Hollande. It was all caught on both men's cameras, the action, the moment's a pathos and sacrifice. It would play well. But the questions raised by the investigation of that meat locker on board the shipwrecked luxury liner vexed her and the men of Explorer II. Still, they were getting their shipmates back. The sea was returning them rather than taking them this time. They were jubilant about this, but it was too soon to celebrate. That must wait until both men were firmly on the deck of the Explorer.

Jim's confused thoughts as he ascended began to coalesce and in his mind's eye, he again saw what he'd witnessed inside the galley at that freezer door as it began to close on Dolph. There were a gaggle of other divers pushing the door closed. He'd at first begun to shout for them to stop, thinking them divers from the excursion boats unaware of Dolph's being inside. But then he saw there were others, people in street clothes and no diving equipment whatsoever, and there was the little girl, a child of perhaps eleven or twelve in a taffeta dress telling them all to close the door.

It was how Thom Pritchards had gone to his Maker. It could as well have been Jim or Dolph as well. But who were those people doing the bidding of that child? And who were those bodies dangling in the freezer? How did they fit into this nightmare?

At the same time as Jim Hollande was trying desperately to sort out his nightmare from reality and reality from his nightmare, Dolph Nielsen was lamenting the death of his friend and colleague Professor Thom Pritchards.

Nielsen's clear thoughts as he ascended focused on the ghosts of another era altogether. Enrico Fermi, clever choice if you wanted the genes of a genius. Then there were the other three, Hugo Eckener, Siegfried Handloser, and Inge Viermetz – all four exemplary geniuses in their fields. The Chosen People to reinvigorate a science to create Hitler's dream of a master race. The dream still very much alive somewhere in America.

Pritchards' had developed a theory of why the Andrea Doria was intentionally rammed the night of July 25,1956. It had been an attempt to end once and for all the ugly work of American Neo-Nazis who had plans to see the 4th Reich rise from the ashes of the 3rd by creating a new and better Fuhrer, and they planned to do it in California.

As crazy as it seemed, it appeared that Professor Pritchards had been right. With the hour-long ascent becoming a bore, it was not long before

111

Dolph began to think over some of the facts first imparted to him by Professor Pritchards, the history expert.

Eugenics had been born as a scientific curiosity in the Victorian age. In 1863, Sir Francis Galton, Charles Darwin's cousin, theorized that if talented people only married other talented people, the result would be measurably better offspring. At the turn of the last century, Galton's ideas were imported into the United States just as Gregor Mendel's principles of heredity were rediscovered. American eugenic advocates believed with religious fervor that the same Mendelian concepts determining the color and size of peas, corn and cattle also governed the social and intellectual character of mankind.

Dolph had been a young man when he had first encountered Professor Pritchards in his classroom. The man was so passionate about this awful stain on his country. Dolph could hear the compassion in the professor's voice when he insisted on lecturing about it, the lecture that had gotten him his walking papers and pension. Dolph thought of those words now:

"In an America reeling from immigration upheaval and torn by post-Reconstruction chaos, race conflict was everywhere. Elitists, utopians and so-called progressives fused their smoldering race fears and class bias with their desire to make a better world. They reinvented Galton's eugenics into a repressive and racist ideology. The intent: populate the earth with vastly more of their own

112

socio-economic and biological kind—and to end with fewer to none of every other kind.

The superior species the eugenics movement sought were to be populated not merely by tall, strong, talented people. Eugenicists craved blond, blue-eyed Nordic types. This group alone, they believed, was fit to inherit the earth. In the process, the movement intended to subtract emancipated Negroes, immigrant Asian laborers, Indians, Hispanics, East Europeans, Jews, dark-haired hill folk, poor people, the infirm and really anyone classified outside the gentrified genetic lines drawn up by American raceologists."

How? By identifying so-called "defective" family trees and subjecting them to lifelong segregation and sterilization programs to kill their bloodlines. The grand plan was to literally wipe away the reproductive capability of those deemed weak and inferior. The so-called "unfit." The eugenicists hoped to neutralize the viability these unfit races 100 percent, until no race was left except themselves.

Eighteen solutions were explored in a Carnegie-supported 1911 Preliminary Report of the Committee of the Eugenic Section of the American Breeder's Association to Study and to Report on the Best Practical Means for Cutting Off the Defective Germ-Plasm in the Human Population. Point eight was euthanasia.

The most commonly suggested method of eugenicide in America was a "lethal chamber" or public locally operated gas chambers. In 1918,

113

Popenoe, the Army venereal disease specialist during World War I, co-wrote the widely used textbook, Applied Eugenics, which argued, "From an historical point of view, the first method which presents itself is execution... Its value in keeping up the standard of the race should not be underestimated." Applied Eugenics also devoted a chapter to Lethal Selection, which operated "through the destruction of the individual by some adverse feature of the environment, such as excessive cold, or bacteria, or by bodily deficiency."

But Dolph wondered what was going on in 1956 and what connection did the four corpses deep and hidden in the bowels of Andrea Doria have to do with eugenics? Professor Pritchards must have had a clue, but what had it been?

Eugenic breeders believed American society was not ready to implement an organized lethal solution. But many mental institutions and doctors practiced improvised medical lethality and passive euthanasia on their own. One institution in Lincoln, Illinois fed its incoming patients milk from tubercular cows believing a eugenically strong individual would be immune. Thirty to forty percent annual death rates resulted at Lincoln. Some doctors practiced passive eugenicide one newborn infant at a time. Others doctors at mental institutions engaged in lethal neglect.

Nonetheless, with eugenicide marginalized, the main solution for eugenicists was the rapid expansion of forced segregation and sterilization, as well as more marriage restrictions. California led

114

the nation, performing nearly all sterilization procedures with little or no due process. In its first twenty-five years of eugenic legislation, California sterilized 9,782 individuals, mostly women. Many were classified as "bad girls," diagnosed as "passionate," "oversexed" or "sexually wayward." At Sonoma, some women were sterilized because of what was deemed an abnormally large clitoris or labia.

In 1933 alone, at least 1,278 coercive sterilizations were performed, 700 of which were on women. The state's two leading sterilization mills in 1933 were Sonoma State Home with 388 operations and Patton State Hospital with 363 operations. Other sterilization centers included Agnews, Mendocino, Napa, Norwalk, Stockton and Pacific Colony state hospitals.

Finally, Dolph could see above and beyond Jim Hollande the surface. Jim had improved as he went, had gotten stronger. Wanted to live. All good signs. Dolph wanted to live as well, and he had the vague since that while he had saved Jim's life, Jim's having hung back for whatever reason had saved Dolph's life as well.

Once safely aboard Explorer II, Jim had changed. He was quiet, moody, not wishing to be touched, not even by Jenna. He was standoffish, shaky, and he had the look of a newborn deer or giraffe when he tried to stand. He lost his legs and fell back to the deck. The others tried to help him remove his gear, and he fought them, saying he was all right and that he could manage. He was terribly out of sorts. He'd wanted to return the conquering hero, impressing everyone, especially Jenna, having discovered Pritchards' remains. But all of it fell to Dolph instead. It was a bitter disappointment in this regard.

Jake grabbed his hand and shook it, pumping hard until Jim snatched it away, Jake saying, "You're a brave if stupid fellow, Jim, and you almost got yourself and Dolph killed but you waited for him. You proved yourself a good man, a good partner to have. Now tell us, what did you see moving that door?"

Jim stared at Jake for a long moment. Then he looked from face to face, finally resting on Dolph who'd begun getting out of Jakes dive suit. "What are you talking about, Jake?" asked Dolph.

"Something had a hand on that door, pushing it closed on you, Dolph, and it wasn't Jim here. It was something unseen by the cameras, but Jim, you saw it."

Jim gritted his teeth and finally described what he had seen at the door. Jenna said, "It's the same specters I saw in the ballroom and their little master, Lorena. She must have such a strong hold on the souls of those she entices into her eternal home."

"She was there all right, and she was working hard to get at least one of us, Dolph, and I couldn't do a damn thing about it."

"That's all right, partner," said Dolph. "In the end, we helped one another out of there. The things I saw inside that freezer will haunt me."

116

"About the things we all saw inside the freezer," said Jenna. "Those carcasses were real and they're caught on camera, along with Pritchards' remains."

"I really wanted to drag him out of there. My old friend."

"So you came on this expedition under false pretenses," said Jake.

"I wanted what you all wanted, yes. The professor was my mentor in many ways."

"I think we need to let these men gather their senses, shower, change, and rest," said Sam in a take-charge tone. "At mess tonight, we're going to want to hear the whole story, Mr. Nielsen."

Dolph nodded appreciatively, and he and Jim went in search of their berths, towels, soap, and rest. The others talked among themselves. Things had hardly gone as planned. Things on board the Explorer were awry.

At dinner, all present, Dolph got right to what was on everyone's mind. "Not many people know or wish to recognize that the master Nordic race didn't originate with Hitler. That in fact, the idea was created in the United States, and cultivated in California, decades before Hitler came to power."

"California eugenicists, yes," said Jake. 'They played an important, although little known, role in the American eugenics movement's campaign for ethnic cleansing."

Sam shrugged and asked, "What the hell're you two talking about?"

117

Dolph calmly explained, saying, "Eugenics was the racist pseudo-science determined to wipe away all human beings deemed unfit, preserving only those who conformed to a Nordic stereotype."

"Like you and every man depicted on romance novel covers?" asked Jenna.

Jim smirked at this.

Dolph continued, ignoring the aside. "Elements of the philosophy were enshrined as national policy by forced sterilization and segregation laws, as well as marriage restrictions, enacted in twenty-seven states. In 1909, California became the third state to adopt such laws."

"That's crazy," said Jim. "Lies."

Jake put up a hand to Jim. "Unfortunately, Jim, Jake, it's another inconvenient truth."

Dolph added, "Ultimately, eugenics practitioners coercively sterilized some 60,000 Americans, barred the marriage of thousands, forcibly segregated thousands in so-called colonies, and persecuted untold numbers in ways we are just learning. Before World War II, nearly half of coercive sterilizations were done in California, and even after the war, the state accounted for a third of all such surgeries."

Jake sighed heavily and said, "California was considered an epicenter of the American eugenics movement. During the Twentieth Century's first decades, California's eugenicists included potent but little known race scientists, such as Army venereal disease specialists."

"Yes, Jake, such as Dr. Paul Popenoe, citrus magnate and Polytechnic benefactor Paul Gosney, Sacramento banker Charles M. Goethe, as well as members of the California State Board of Charities and Corrections and the University of California Board of Regents."

"This is crazy and what's it got to do with the Andrea Doria?" asked Jim.

"Getting to that," replied Dolph. "Look, Eugenics would have been so much bizarre parlor talk had it not been for extensive financing by corporate philanthropies, specifically the Carnegie Institution, the Rockefeller Foundation, and the Harriman railroad fortune."

"I've read about it extensively, Jim," Jake assured the others. "They were all in league with some of America's most respected scientists."

"Men hailing from prestigious universities in America. Stamford, Yale, Harvard, and Princeton. These academicians espoused race theory and race science, and then faked and twisted data to serve eugenics' racist aims.

"It was Stanford president David Starr Jordan who originated the notion of race and blood in his 1902 in his super racially charged epistle 'Blood of a Nation' in which he declared that human qualities and conditions such as talent and poverty were passed through the blood."

"This...all this was at a time when people were ignorant," Jenna put in.

"Pritchards feared the thinking was still with many Americans today, and many in state and

119

federal positions. If he could prove it was still rampant in 1956, he could make a case that it still persists in American politics and culture." This had all eyes on Dolph.

"You're Norwegian, so why should you care?" asked Jim.

"Jim, Jim, all of you," countered Jake. "In 1904, the Carnegie Institution established a laboratory complex at Cold Spring Harbor on Long Island that stockpiled millions of index cards on ordinary Americans, as researchers carefully plotted the removal of families, bloodlines and whole peoples. From Cold Spring Harbor, eugenics advocates agitated in state legislatures across America, as well as the nation's social service agencies and associations."

"Let me answer Jim's question for you all. Why should I care? I am not an American. I care because I loved that old man, Pritchards and what he stood for, and what he was trying to do on the Andrea Doria, and he came so close."

Jake then said, "The Harriman railroad fortune paid local charities like the New York Bureau of Industries and Immigration to seek out Jewish, Italian and other immigrants in New York and other crowded cities to subject them to deportation, trumped up confinement, or forced sterilization."

"Add to that the Rockefeller Foundation," said Dolph. "They helped found the German eugenics program and even funded the program that Josef Mengele worked in before he went to Auschwitz."

"This is too much," said Jenna.

"Much of the spiritual guidance and political agitation for the American eugenics movement came from California's quasi-autonomous eugenic societies," Jakes said with a shrug. "Pasadena-based Human Betterment Foundation and the California branch of the American Eugenics Society."

"All of which coordinated activity with the Eugenics Research Society in Long Island. These organizations functioned as part of a closely-knit network."

"They published racist eugenic newsletters and pseudoscientific journals, such as Eugenics and Eugenical News and, and propagandized for the Nazis."

"I think I've heard all I can stomach of this," said Jenna. "It's awful."

"Doesn't fit your documentary, you mean," said Dolph.

"Now that's not fair!" she argued.

"But Dolph's right. This does throw a monkey wrench in. Changes the whole facts and tone of what we've discovered about the Andrea Doria. Someone placed those corpses in that freezer compartment, and it had to be pretty high-level."

"Are we going to chance another dive?" asked Sharky. "Get Pritchards out of that tomb and home—our initial reason for being here?"

"We go back, we risk becoming one of them. Them being those trapped down there."

"I'm thinking we leave a tomb alone," said Jim. "I mean with what we know, what we have all seen. I should have listened to you all when you told me, but I didn't believe it until I saw it with my own eyes."

"But if we just leave, do nothing, bury the footage," said Jake, "then it's all been for nothing."

"There's one more consideration," Jenna said.

"Which is?" asked Jake.

"If we can free those trapped souls down there…I mean if I can lead Lenora out of that shipwreck and into the light…"

"What light? There's no light down there. None but ours."

"Then we use our lights. Sharky, you have that Army flash, strongest ever made?" she asked.

"Sure I do."

"We put it over the side, guide Leonora to the surface, and she'll find he light, and she'll be free after all these years."

"What about the others like the gone divers' souls?"

"I have a theory that they are only held in the wreck due to Lenora's power over them. She is the key. We get her out and up, the others will be free."

"All save those in the freezer?" asked Dolph. "I want to get Pritchards' remains back to his family as much as the rest of you, and not for any reward."

"And what of the four on the meat hooks? Those aren't spirits but corpses," said Jim.

"Someone on the Stockholm went to great trouble and killed some fifty innocent people to put those corpses there," said Dolph. "Perhaps we should leave them to their tomb."

122

"And when another diver finds them?" asked Jaked. "No…no we need to tell the world about this…this ugly discovery. I want us all to agree on that score."

"I'm with you, Jake," said Sharky without hesitation. "Me too," said Dolph, "if that's what you all want.

"All right, but it all goes into the documentary, Jake—all of it. The good, the bad, and the ugly."

Jake nodded. "What about you, Jim? You all in?"

Jim only hesitated a moment. "We're going to make history. Shake up a few foundations, yeah. All in."

Sharky told them all they had a couple more hours before they could dive, and that Jim and Dolph had a great deal more hours before they could go down, so Jim would be manning the control room again when, after everyone got some rest, the original team would drop below.

One more dive to that dangerous place that got under the skin. One more to bring Lenora to the light…clear the wreck of ghosts…. bring up Pritchards on a lowered platform…but what of the four horsemen of the Apocalypse—as Jake had called the strange group of dead men on meat hooks. The same ones that Thom Pritchard had died seeking. The same four that Dolph Nielsen had discovered with Jim Hollande's help?

These considerations did not allow for much sleep or mindful rest. Jenna feared she was not the only one unable to sleep. They had come extremely close to losing Jim and Dolph below. They'd been lucky, and she had been lucky in learning precisely what was going on below, sure now that young Lenora held the key to it all. She wanted to suit up now, get underway. She got up from her attempt to do as Sharky had said, paced the small cabin, found it not roomy enough for pacing, and instead went topside, found a lounge used by the crew and tried to sleep to the rocking boat and the sound of waves lapping at the boat.

Jake Stoughton was having his own challenge to find sleep. He couldn't get the strange turn of events out of his mind. Ironically, he'd done his dissertation on America's Eugenics Programs when he was working toward his BS degree, a long time ago. But he recalled the ugly facts. Even the United States Supreme Court had endorsed aspects of eugenics. In the court's infamous 1927 decision, Justice Oliver Wendell Holmes had written something to the effect that it'd be best "for all the world, if instead of waiting to execute degenerate offspring for crime, or to let them starve for their imbecility, society can prevent those who are manifestly unfit from continuing their kind." He'd added, "Three generations of imbeciles are enough."

That decision opened the floodgates for thousands to be coercively sterilized or otherwise persecuted as subhuman. Years later, the Nazis at the Nuremberg trials quoted Holmes's words in their own defense.

Only after eugenics became entrenched in the United States was the campaign transplanted into Germany, in no small measure through the efforts of California eugenicists. So-called superior people who published booklets idealizing sterilization, and who'd circulated them to German officials and scientists.

Hitler studied American eugenics laws. He 'legitimized' his anti-Semitism by medicalizing it, by wrapping it in the more palatable pseudo-scientific facade of eugenics. Hitler, now able to recruit more followers among reasonable Germans by claiming that science was on his side, saw his race hatred triple and quadruple.

While Hitler's personal race hatred sprung from his own mind, the intellectual outlines of the eugenics that Hitler adopted in 1924 were made in America.

During the '20s, Carnegie Institution eugenic scientists cultivated deep personal and professional relationships with Germany's fascist eugenicists. In Hitler's Mein Kampf, published in 1924, Hitler quoted American eugenic ideology and openly displayed a thorough knowledge of American eugenics.

Jake struggled to recall Adolph Hitler's exact line word for word: There is today one state in which at least weak beginnings toward a better conception of immigration are noticeable. Of course, it is not our model German Republic, but the United States.

Hitler had proudly told comrades just how closely he followed the progress of the American eugenics movement. He'd confided to one fellow Nazi, "I've studied with great interest the laws of several American states concerning prevention of reproduction by people whose progeny would, in all probability, be of no value or be injurious to the racial stock."

Hitler even wrote a fan letter to American eugenic leader Madison Grant in which he named Grant's race-based eugenics book, The Passing of the Great Race "My bible."

Recalling all of his research now, Jake could find no REM sleep. He pushed off from his berth, slipped on a shirt and khaki's and went topside where he found a wakeful Jenna.

"You, too, eh?" she said as he approached.

"Hard to sleep with so much going on. I mean this, kiddo, all of it, is beyond belief, and yet it's happening before our eyes."

"Do you think Dolph Nielsen knew more going in than the rest of us?"

Jake chuckled. "Are you kidding? We went down there like so many babes, bent on finding Pritchards without the least notion of what the man was looking for down there when he obviously found it and died for his troubles."

"You're right, and Dolph knew his reasoning."

Jake shared what he knew of Hitler's admiration of the American Eugenics Movement leaders with Jenna. "Hitler's struggle for a superior race morphed into his mad crusade for a Master

Race. Now, the American term Nordic was freely exchanged with Germanic or Aryan. Race science, racial purity and racial dominance became the driving force behind Hitler's Nazism. Nazi eugenics would ultimately dictate who would be persecuted in a Reich-dominated Europe, how people would live, and how they would die."

She nodded throughout what Jake was saying, then said, "Nazi doctors became the unseen generals in Hitler's war against the Jews."

"And other Europeans deemed inferior."

Jake eased in beside her on a lounge chair beside her. Jenna thoughtfully said, "Then it was doctors who created the science of extermination and genocide."

"They certainly devised the eugenic formulas, and even hand-selected the victims for sterilization, euthanasia and mass extermination."

They sat in silence for a long moment, the ocean lapping at the boat, a reminder of who they were, why they were here 250 feet above the Andrea Doria, when Sharky joined them. Sam too was unable to sleep. He'd heard their voices and had heard the last of what they were discussing. He joined in, knowing something of the subject himself.

"During the Reich's early years, eugenicists across America welcomed Hitler's plans as the logical fulfillment of their own decades of research and effort. California eugenicists republished Nazi propaganda for American consumption. They also arranged for Nazi scientific exhibits."

"That's right," said Jake. "I think it was fall, August maybe 1934, they displayed some shit at the L.A. County Museum, for the annual meeting of the American Public Health Association."

By then Germany's sterilizations were accelerating beyond 5,000 per month," said Sam.

Jake nodded and said, "T, he California eugenics leader, guy named Goethe returned from Germany bragging to his friends about how the work in the U.S. was playing a big role in shaping the opinions of intellectuals behind Hitler."

"Said something along the lines of, 'Our work here has jolted into action the great government of 60 million people."

"Shameful that America provided the scientific roadmap to the Holocaust," Jenna said.

"Even more shameful, America funded Germany's eugenic institutions," said Dolph who joined the group now on deck. From where he leaned against the rail, he added, "By 1926, Rockefeller had donated some $410,000, that's like $4 million in 21st Century money, to hundreds of German researchers. In May 1926, Rockefeller awarded $250,000 to the German Psychiatric Institute of the Kaiser Wilhelm Institute, later to become the Kaiser Wilhelm Institute for Psychiatry. Among the leading psychiatrists at the German Psychiatric Institute was Ernst Rüdin, who became director and eventually an architect of Hitler's systematic medical repression."

"It's so horrible," said Jenna. "Shakes my faith in…in everything."

Dolph shrugged, and Jake muttered, "Man's inhumanity to man."

Sam paced the deck, silent.

Dolph continued, saying, "Then, too, there was the Institute for Brain Research. Since 1915, it'd operated out of a single room. Everything changed when Rockefeller money arrived in 1929. A grant of $317,000 allowed the Institute to construct a major building and take center stage in German race biology. The Institute received additional grants from the Rockefeller Foundation during the next several years. Leading the Institute, once again, was Hitler's medical henchman Ernst Rüdin."

Jake jumped in with, "Rüdin's organization became a prime director and recipient of the murderous experimentation and research conducted on Jews, Gypsies and others."

"That's right," replied Dolph. "Beginning in 1940, between fifty to one-hundred thousand Germans were taken from old age homes, mental institutions, and other custodial facilities. No one ever saw them again; they were systematically gassed."

"I remember some guy from my research that I'd quoted for my dissertation," said Jake. "Don't recall his name, an exec with the American Eugenics Society talking about the Nazis, saying, 'While we're pussy-footing around...the Germans are calling a spade a spade."

Everyone fell silent for a short interval. The sea breeze picked up and washed over them. Jim Hollande joined them. "Couldn't sleep," he needn't have said. "This a powwow about the next dive?" he asked.

"Talking about the Nazis and American eugenics, Jim," Jenna replied.

Jim took up a spot along the rail, staring off into the sea as the sun was rising in the east, creating a beautiful line of gold there and painting the clouds in fifty shades of pink.

Dolph broke the silence, saying, "A special recipient of Rockefeller funding was the Kaiser Wilhelm Institute for Anthropology, Human Heredity and Eugenics in Berlin. For decades, American eugenicists had craved twins to advance their research into heredity. The Institute was now prepared to undertake such research on an unprecedented level. In 1932, the Rockefeller Foundation in New York dispatched a radiogram to its Paris office about a June meeting of their executive committee. Nine thousand dollars over a three-year period for research on twins and the effects on later generations of substances toxic for germ plasm."

"I think we've all heard enough," Jenna now said, getting up from her lounge chair and joining Hollande at the rail to share the sunset.

"But you haven't heard about all the dots that tie it all to Italy and the use of ships like the Andrea Doria to transport genetic materials in the form of bodies, have you?" asked Dolph of the group. "Something that may well still be going on. 1956 was not so long ago."

130

Jake grimly added, "Not the sort of thing you see on the social calendar while on a cruise."

CHAPTER NINE

I am just waiting for you,
for an interval somewhere very near,
just around the corner...All is well.

Not even Juan, the cook, had gotten a good night's sleep, and he hit the buzzer that signaled breakfast was ready in the galley for those who wanted it. They had another hour before anyone could dive, so the crew reassembled in the galley. Once served and having coffee, Jake said to Dolph, "Why don't you enlighten us, Dolph."

Dolph swallowed his coffee and began. "At the time of Rockefeller's endowment, Otmar Freiherr von Verschuer, a hero in American eugenics circles, functioned as a head of the Institute for Anthropology, Human Heredity and Eugenics. Rockefeller funding of that Institute continued both directly and through other research conduits during Verschuer's early tenure. In 1935, Verschuer left the Institute to form a rival eugenics facility in Frankfurt that was much heralded in the American eugenic press. Research on twins in the Third Reich exploded, backed up by government decrees. Verschuer wrote in Der Erbarzt, a eugenic doctor's journal he edited, that 'Germany's war will yield a total solution to the Jewish problem'.

"How is the Doria involved?" asked an impatient Jim Hollande.

"Getting to that, Jim. Listen to me, Verschuer had a long-time assistant. You may recognize the name: Josef Mengele."

The name chilled the room. Hitler's butcher.

"On May 30, 1943, Mengele arrived at Auschwitz. Verschuer notified the German Research Society in a letter of introduction. Something to the effect that his assistant, Dr. Josef Mengele, M.D., Ph.D. joined him in this branch of research. He is presently employed as Hauptsturmführer – captain and camp physician in the Auschwitz concentration camp. Anthropological testing of the most diverse racial groups in this concentration camp is being carried out with permission of the SS Reichsführer who was Himmler."

"That sonofabitch Mengele began searching the boxcar arrivals for twins right off," said Jake. "And when he found them, he performed beastly experiments, scrupulously wrote up the reports, and sent the paperwork back to Verschuer, right? His institute for evaluation?"

"Yes, and often along with carefully preserved cadavers, sometimes just the eyes and other body parts. All dispatched to Berlin's eugenic institutes."

"Did Rockefeller executives know of Mengele?" asked Jenna.

Dolph shook his head. "With few exceptions, the foundation had ceased all eugenic studies in Nazi-occupied Europe before the war erupted in 1939. But by that time the die had been cast. The talented men Rockefeller and Carnegie financed, the

133

institutions they helped found, and the science it helped create took on a scientific momentum of its own."

Jake put in a word, saying, "After the war, eugenics was declared a crime against humanity—an act of genocide. Germans were tried and they cited the California statutes in their defense. To no avail. They were found guilty as sin—as they should have."

"However, Mengele's boss Verschuer escaped prosecution. The SOB re-established his connections with California eugenicists who had gone underground and renamed their crusade Human Genetics. Soon, Verschuer once again became a respected scientist in Germany and around the world. In 1949, he became a corresponding member of the newly formed American Society of Human Genetics, organized by American eugenicists and geneticists."

"Holy shit. The snake slithered off into the grass, eh?" said Sam Kent, shaking his shaggy head.

"It gets worse," said Dolph. "In the fall of 1950, the University of Münster offered Verschuer a position at its new Institute of Human Genetics, where he later became a dean. In the early and mid-1950s, Verschuer became an honorary member of numerous prestigious societies, including the Italian Society of Genetics, the Anthropological Society of Vienna, and the Japanese Society for Human Genetics."

The talk of Nazi and US eugenics and cadavers was put aside for the day's dive plan. Everyone had to be clear and exacting about what each job was and how much air and time it would all take. Their first concern, and everyone agreed, was to free Thom Pritchards of his watery tomb. The second concern was to free the spirit of the child, but to safely get Pritchards onto a platform lowered to the ship and raised, they must deal with the specter of Lorena Morgan. She would certainly impede any attempt to raise the body if she was not dealt with. Since all of those present had had some dealings with the eerie hauntings below, no one disputed Jenna's reasoning.

Their plan must begin with Jenna contacting the child and helping her to the light which would be beamed down to the shipwreck. With Jenna distracting the ghost, the other two divers, Jake and Sam would enter the freezer and retrieve Thom Pritchards' body, get him out to the platform and signal for a hoist. Knowing this would take all the time they had inside and hovering over the Andrea Doria, they had no hope of getting all of the other cadavers onto the platform. Possibly one, but certainly not all four. It would be a trial dive to see how long it would take to get Pritchards' corpse and possibly Enrico Fermi's body out. On a subsequent dive, hopefully without the problem of Lorena Morgan, Jim Hollande and Dolph Nielsen might possibly get the last three corpses onto the platform and raise the dead of Doria.

Now it was time. Jenna was first over the side. Immediately using her psychic abilities, the moment she entered the water, she called out to Lorena by name, interchanging her name with baby, honey, and other endearments. She meant to be a surrogate mother to the child for the duration of this dive while the men worked to free Pritchards.

As she descended, she made the plea for Lorena to give her full attention to Jenna. She promised an escape to heaven, and she promised an escape to a place where there was an even bigger and more beautiful dance floor, perfect for a princess like Lorena.

Second over the side was Jake, quickly followed by Sam. Regardless of their restless night, the adrenaline was flowing. In the control room, all three were being monitored by Jim and Dolph. The cameras were rolling; the documentation of every move was on. The documentary would be made come hell or high water, regardless of who it might touch as no one on board knew how high up this conspiracy went. All they knew for sure was that human genetic study had its roots in eugenics, and that so much had been ignored since 1959 by generations of Americans who refused to link America with the crimes of Nazism, and the succeeding generations that simply did not know the truth about the years leading up to WWII and the Holocaust.

While it was now true that governors of five U.S. states, including California had issued public apologies to their citizens, past and present, for sterilization and other abuses spawned by the eugenics movement, most people did not associate these horrible programs with Nazi genocide and Nazi experimentation on humans.

Besides, human genetics had become an enlightened endeavor by the late twentieth century. Hard-working, devoted scientists had finally cracked the human code through the Human Genome Project. Now, every individual on Earth could be biologically identified and classified by trait and ancestry. Yet even now, some leading voices in the genetic world were calling for a cleansing of the unwanted among us, and even a master human species.

There remained understandable wariness about the mundane, ordinary forms of abuse, for example, in denying insurance or employment based on genetic tests. On October 14, 2008 America's first genetic anti-discrimination legislation passed the Senate by unanimous vote. But genetics research also remained global, no single nation's law could put a stop the threat of a frame of mind that secretly or openly proposed a return to Nazi eugenics.

The descent to the shipwreck went smoothly as the team had boarded the platform to be lowered down, and they rode upon it, the three of them saving precious air as a result since they were not using up energy.

Once over the wreck, they went for the now familiar path to the galley they'd all been calling Sam's trek. Once inside the galley, the men worked

137

with crowbars and muscle to get the freezer door reopened. Pulling against the pressure of the trapped ocean water was no easy task, and for a while it appeared a nearly impossible one. The men pried and pulled only to create a sliver of an opening so far.

Jenna went into an altered state of consciousness, knowing it was her only chance at bringing Lenora to her in order to communicate. As soon as she had gone into trance, Sam and Jim from above were shouting for the men to see to her, that her vital signs had gone precipitously down.

Dolph started for Jenna, but Jake grabbed him, hand-signaling to keep working on the door and to not stop. He said over the com-link, "She's communicating with the dead. Let her be."

Dolph reluctantly turned his attention back to the door. The opening had widened little by little. The men could fit through now, but it would be difficult getting out with Pritchards' body and Fermi's as it was. They worked to open the door wider against the pressure. Once they were happy with the result, the door halfway open, Jake shoved a loose pipe into place to hold it open, and they entered the freezer compartment.

They soon had hold of Thom Pritchards and were together easing his remains out and toward Sam's trek for the platform outside the wreck. Both men looked back at Jenna who was staring at something unseen ahead of her.

"I'm worried for her, Jake," Dolph said. "She could become the eighteenth diver the Doria claims."

"She's tougher than she looks, Dolph. We have to stick to the plan if any of this is going to work."

"Trust that she can bring about a change in the dead girl, you mean?"

"Exactly what I mean."

Once outside, they saw the incredible beam of light that sluiced through the sea from above at the Explorer. The light somehow gave both men hope and trust in the plan. They quickly boarded Pritchards' remains, lashing the body to the platform, and once this effort was complete, checking their gauges, the pair rushed back for the galley and the freezer for the first of the secreted cadavers on board the Andrea Doria for sixty some odd years.

Once Jake and Dolph were back, they passed Jenna for the second time. She looked like a statue. From up above, the men expressed more concern for her. Jake said firmly to Sam, "She's doing her thing, Sam, and your noise only makes it impossible, so shut up! You too, Jim."

Jake punched Dolph in the arm to keep him moving. Their time was limited and getting more limited by the second. As they entered the freezer a second time, Jake looked back at the frozen Jenna and secretly was as worried for her as anyone. He imagined her in a war of wills with the dead Morgan girl. No doubt, he told himself but focused on the job at hand.

He and Dolph worked to get the body of Enrico Fermi down from the huge hook spiked into his skull at the base of the brain. "They sure weren't planning to revive Enrico, now were they?" said Jake as they struggled to get the corpse free.

Success, the cadaver was free, and they began moving it out like a stiff log. The hoarfrost covering the entire frame and facial features cracked like glass.

The two divers talked calmly as they moved Fermi's remains out and past Jenna, who was as yet unmoved.

"I don't believe those behind this believe in cryogenics could ever see whole bodies and minds rejuvenated. Not precisely in that way," replied Dolph. "However, their aim is more in line with cellular work, genetic cloning, harvesting of genes in the lab."

"Bastards. Do you think it's still going on…you know covertly, in America?"

"America, Germany, Italy, possibly other countries involved, yes. I fear so, yes."

"You're not really a ship's engineer, are you, Dolph?"

"Well, I do have those skills."

"But you're what, CIA, FBI?"

"Norway's equivalent of your CIA. The Stockholm was always suspect. I started digging years ago."

They got the second body out and onto the platform. Jake told Dolph to go, ride it up…keep it steady. Sam will know at what intervals to stop your progress on ascent."

"What about you and Jenna?"

"I'm going back for her now. Obviously, she's not been successful in her efforts."

Dolph gave him an underwater high-five, and then spoke directly to Sam about hoisting the bodies with him on the platform up. As the platform began upwards, Dolph saw the last of Jake's fins disappear into the hull of the ship. He gave a silent prayer for Jake and Jenna.

"One more dive, we get the last three in the meat locker out," Jim said from above.

Knowing they could get two out in the time it had taken, having had the practice, three now would be no problem, so long as Jake and Jenna returned safely.

Inside the galley again, Jake approached Jenna with the notion to get her out now. He had no idea if she'd had any success whatsoever, but their time here was pretty close to nil. Jake reached out to give her a stiff shake, when suddenly she moved away from his fingertips. She had not seen his return, and she moved forward, deeper into the death trap this place was becoming for them. He called out to her, but she was calling out to Lenora. She was calling the girl's name in a chanting fashion, not wishing to give up.

Jake could wait no longer. He raced through the murky water and grabbed Jenna, forcing her to come with him, but when they turned toward Sam's

141

exit, Jake and Jenna could both see that it was blocked by a crowd of ghosts, some wearing dive suits.

"We go through them, Jenna, now!"

But before the ghosts now Lorena materialized. She had been listening all along. She had come to Jenna. "Follow us out, Jenna, into the light. Go to your real heaven and away from this place. Come, follow us to the light."

"We're dead here too, Jenna, if we don't start up for the light ourselves." Jake nudged her onward. Lorena's image disappeared as did the crowd blocking their way.

"She says we can go, Jake."

"Tell her we'll be back for her. Come on."

"Come with us baby girl, child," Jenna said aloud now what she had been saying psychically since their arrival. "You free yourself and all those here with you, they will be free, too."

Jake ushered her along the promenade now where one after another of Lorena's ghosts came rushing at them only to rush through them. Once above the ship, going for the strobe lights they'd placed on the guide rope, something made Jenna pull away from Jake and turn. Jake cursed and turned back to grab her again when he saw the specter of the lost sister, the child more fully formed than ever before. Lorena was floating in the sea and moving up and up toward the promised light.

Jenna breathed a sigh of relief on seeing this sight. Jake stared in awe as well at the closest thing he'd ever seen to an angel.

142

As Lenora's image rose, getting closer and closer to the light, soon bathed in the light, she dissipated somewhere near the surface.

Jake snatched Jenna out of her reverie over the child and got her to the tether, urging her up ahead of him. The pair began their ascent, their hearts full. Their dive had been more successful than they could have dreamed.

Epilogue

I am just waiting for you,
for an interval somewhere very near,
just around the corner...All is well.

With Jenna, Jake, and Dolph all back on board Explorer II, the next dive had Sam and Jim going down to the galley and heading into the freezer. They worked quickly and efficiently, and they had wisely brought with them duplicate tanks so that they could remain longer at the wreck to retrieve the final three bodies found in the freezer. Each frozen stiff corpse was placed on the platform and tied securely like so much cord wood. With all three ready, Sam gave the OK for the platform to be hoisted up. He and Jim then went for the tether line to make their much slower ascent to the surface.

As they rose up from the shipwreck, Jim thought he saw shadows, movement through the row of broken windows along the promenade deck. Perhaps his eyes were playing tricks on him, perhaps not. Then he and Sam saw the giant squid rise of from behind the ship and crawl across the deck, squat there and rest like a sentinel. Was it guarding the ship against future divers? Or was it guarding the spirits within?

The pair of divers were just pleased that the creature chose to remain stationary there. It was large enough to swallow either or both of them should it get its tentacles around a man.

The rest of the ascent went off without incident, and Jim's camera had picked up the sight of the giant squid where it hovered about the Andrea Doria. Jenna, seeing it from above at the control room, at first gasped, but then she said, "This will make a great shot in our film, Jake."

Jake smiled at this. "I'm sure it will."

Dolph and Jake stepped away from Jenna and quietly discussed what must be done next. They both agreed that they knew not who to trust. "We can't trust the US government or officials," said Jake. "What about Norway? Sweden?"

"No…they'd most likely want to see it buried as well. Someone on board the Stockholm that night in 1956 wanted it buried, and the Swedish government is not likely to want the truth of how the Doria was intentionally rammed now any more than then."

"Sure can't take it to the Italian government."

"We take it to the press—the news media," said Jake. "I have contacts at both the Washington Post and the New York Times."

Dolph Nielsen considered this, nodding. "Yes, the world should be informed. We release it to the press in Norway and Sweeden as well. Coordinate the date and time."

Jenna, overhearing this, said, "That's a great idea. Think of the publicity we'll all get, Jake, and the donations pouring in. Won't hurt the chances for my realty dive show either."

An hour and ten minutes had passed since the platform had been raised, and the fourth body from the freezer had been put on ice on the Explorer. Sam surfaced and made his way on board with Jake helping him do so."

When Sam came on, he asked, "Where's Jim?"

Jenna had rushed out to say, "Jim's fallen away from the tether!"

"He was right behind me!" shouted Sam, his dive equipment still on his back. He pulled away from the others and dropped over the side in search of Jim Hollande. Dolph was suiting up, going in after Sam.

"What's happened?" Jenna wondered aloud.

"Likely the bends got him."

"Or that damned monster squid rose up and grabbed him." Dolph grabbed a spear gun and was over the side.

"God, we could lose them all down there," Jenna said, fighting back a panic attack.

"There is some power surrounding that shipwreck that goes beyond Lenora Morgan's spirit, perhaps," Jake said.

Then suddenly, Sam reappeared alongside Dolph, and both men had a hold of Hollande who was choking for air. "He lost consciousness, rebreather was dangling loose," shouted Sam.

"Just floating at about ten feet."

Soon they were all safely back on board, and Jake was giving CPR to Jim, who soon came around. Everyone was relieved.

"I saw something just before I blacked out," Jim said while still lying on his back.

"What? What'd you see?"

"That ghost girl, that Lenora."

"But she's gone, Jim," Jenna assured him. "We saw her go into the light. She surfaced and her soul was released."

"No…no, she's gone back. She didn't make it all the way. She took me by surprise. One second I am fine and I am seeing the bottom of the boat, and the next she's got her face pressed against mine."

"I have to go back down then, convince her to try again," said Jenna.

"No…no more risks, and out time's up here."

"She asked me if I wanted to dance," said Jim, sitting up now, his pale color taking on a warmer hue now. "She put it in my head that I wanted to go back with her, and I was tempted."

"It's over for us, boys and girls," said Jake. "I'm taking Explorer back on time, and I am getting us all out of here now. We've been more than lucky and successful. We've got five corpses on board to deal with as well, one of them being Thom Pritchards, and we've solved Pritchards' mystery for him, at least up to a point. Wise thing now is to move on with life and be thankful we still have our lives."

Jenna nodded. "Sure, sure."

Jake knew she was already plotting part two of the Doria dive for herself and her reality show plans, and he also knew he would not be a part of part two. When they began this venture, he had thoughts about their becoming a couple before the voyage was over. He no longer had such thoughts. Jim Hollande could continue to chase her, but Jake Stoughton would no longer continue to try his best to change her.

"I say we head immediately for shore and put the Andrea Doria behind us," suggested Dolph.

"Smartest thing I've heard in a long while," replied Jake who shook hands with Dolph. The two men had grown to admire one another on this voyage.

Sam agreed with the notion of putting a lot of distance between the Explorer II and the Andrea Doria. Jenna knelt over the still shivering, shaken Jim and held him in her arms while Jake went to the bridge and Dolph to the anchor. Between them, they got the boat turned around and off for port. Jake wondered what kind of impact the revelation of their discovery of Fermi's body and those of the others on the Doria would have on the media, the general public, the feds, and internationally. He knew it would have an impact on history for in historical terms 'Death is Nothing at All'.

THE END